"I'd Like To Proposition You, Emily.

"You're just the kind of woman I'm looking for."

"I beg your pardon!" Emily said frostily.

"Are you for real, lady?" Zack demanded sarcastically. "Or did you walk in here straight off the pages of some Gothic novel?"

Emily stared at him in disbelieving silence for several seconds, then lifted her chin in a way that would make any Gothic heroine be proud and inquired indignantly, "Whatever do you mean by that?"

Zack rolled his eyes. "Lord, woman, will you just listen to yourself! 'Whatever do you mean, sir,' " he mimicked harshly. "Give me a break! No modern woman talks like that. If I didn't know better, I'd think you'd been withering away in some ruin of a castle for the past forty years."

Stung by his cruel accusations, Emily's retort was out before she could stop it. "Thirty years!" she corrected hotly. "I've only been withering away for thirty years!"

Dear Reader,

Welcome to Silhouette Desire! If this is your first Desire novel, I hope it will be the first of many. If you're a regular reader, you already know that you're in for a treat.

Every Silhouette Desire book contains a romance to remember. These stories can be dramatic or humorous... topical or traditional. Each and every one is a love story that is guaranteed to sweep you into a world of passion. The heroines are women with hopes and fears just like yours. And the heroes—watch out! You won't want to read about just one. It will take all six of these strong men to keep you satisfied.

Next month, look for a special treat... six tantalizing heroes you'll want to get to know—and love—in *Men of the World*. These sinfully sexy men are from six different and romantic countries. Each book has the portrait of your hero on the cover, so you won't be able to miss this handsome lineup. Our featured authors are some of the finest: BJ James, Barbara Faith, Jennifer Greene, Lucy Gordon, Kathleen Korbel and Linda Lael Miller. *Men of the World*—don't miss them.

And don't miss September's *Man of the Month* book, *Lone Wolf* by Annette Broadrick. It sizzles!

Happy reading,

Lucia Macro
Senior Editor

JOYCE THIES

PRIDE AND JOY

SILHOUETTE *Desire*®

Published by Silhouette Books New York

America's Publisher of Contemporary Romance

SILHOUETTE BOOKS
300 East 42nd St., New York, N.Y. 10017

PRIDE AND JOY

ISBN: 0-373-05661-3

First Silhouette Books printing September 1991

JOYCE THIES

has been reading and writing romances since her teens but had to wait ten years before one of her books was published. Since then, she has authored or co-authored over twenty contemporary and historical novels. Readers might recognize her as the Joyce half of Janet Joyce. She wrote her first Silhouette Desire novel, *Territorial Rights,* as Melissa Scott, but is now writing under her own name.

She met her husband in college and it was love at first sight. Joyce believes that out of sharing comes growth for both partners. She says, "Because of the loving man in my life, I've become everything I've ever wanted to be: wife, mother and writer. With each book I write, I imagine another woman lucky enough to have it all."

One

Emily Anne Hartcourt was a creature of habit. While in the care of her globe-trotting parents, she'd been much more impetuous and carefree, but once she'd been placed in the hands of her two unmarried aunts, Esther and Ida, and had taken up residence with them at Hartcourt House, she'd learned that adhering to a strict daily schedule greatly simplified her life. Aunt Esther didn't deal well with even a minor upset to her normal routine, and as early as age four, Emily had been so eager to please that she'd swiftly stopped doing upsetting things. Over the following years, she'd developed her own set of habits and, by the age of thirty, had even reached the point where she found a certain comfort in doing the same things at the same time every day.

Although she didn't teach any history classes during the summer quarter at Hensley College, she still rose from her bed at six every morning and was showered and dressed by six-thirty. Years of practice ensured that her unruly brown hair was pinned back off her face in less than three minutes and applying her makeup took even less time than that. Precisely at six forty-one, she seated herself in the breakfast nook to enjoy two pieces of unbuttered whole-wheat toast and a cup of herbal tea while she admired the view of Aunt Ida's well-tended herb garden, which she could see out her kitchen window.

Today, however, as she gazed outside, she wasn't sure she was seeing straight. Normally she paid little attention to the comings and goings of her neighbors, but a low-slung black convertible was parked in the newly paved circular driveway next door, and an extremely short person, wearing what appeared to be a loincloth, was climbing into the passenger seat. Of course Aunt Esther would probably accuse her of gawking, a most unladylike occupation to be sure, but the sight was so unusual, Emily couldn't help staring.

For several seconds, she tried to convince herself that the newest resident on Crabapple Lane was a midget, but then she heard the purr of a powerful engine, and she didn't dare place her entire trust in that farfetched theory. It was much more likely that she was witnessing a small child in an extremely hazardous situation, and that likelihood prompted her to rush out the back door of her house and take off at a dead run across the side yard. Luckily Aunt Esther was still asleep and therefore didn't see her niece vaulting over an azalea bush and thereby revealing a shocking expanse of bare leg.

Emily's first impulse upon arriving at her destination was to reach down and pluck the bright-eyed toddler manning the steering wheel out of harm's way, but the child's cheery greeting stopped her in mid-pluck. "Hi, lady. See? I's driving the Indy 500."

For an instant, Emily reconsidered her midget theory, but then she noted the tiny pink bow attached to a few wispy strands of ultrafine blond hair and realized that no matter what this tiny female person had to say, she was definitely an infant, and young enough to still be in diapers. Since she had absolutely no experience with this particular age group, Emily didn't know how to respond to such an announcement, so she didn't say anything. She did, however, lean over the side of the car, switch off the ignition and pocket the keys, effectively negating any chance the adventuresome child might have had to enter herself in a world-class racing competition.

Her action was instantly rewarded by a high-pitched squeal of indignation and then a series of irate reminders: "I's driving, dammit! I's driving! I's driving!"

As she watched the angry, and unexpectantly profane, toddler jumping up and down on the car's luxurious brown leather seat, Emily felt hopelessly out of her depth. She cast a pleading glance up at the house, but no one came dashing out the front door in response to the commotion taking place in the driveway, so she was left with no choice but to handle the appalling situation herself. "Calm down, baby," she pleaded anxiously. "Please calm down and I'll take you to find your mommy and daddy."

To her astonishment, the child instantly stopped yelling, her big blue eyes lighting up with pleasure as she inquired, "Daddy? You find my daddy?"

Emily nodded reassuringly and the child raised her chubby arms, encouraging Emily to pick her up. "That's a good girl," Emily said, relieved beyond measure as she lifted the now willing child out of the convertible and settled her firmly on her right hip.

"Go find Daddy," the child ordered in an astonishingly imperious tone, and as her rescuer set off toward the house, she murmured, "That's a good lady."

Along with that comment, Emily received an approving pat on the top of her head and, getting the strange feeling she was being patronized, she burst out incredulously, "Just how old are you, anyway?"

The question provoked a fierce scowl and Emily's brows went up at the child's reproachful expression. It was almost as if this young lady, like several other members of her sex, disdained replying to such a rude personal question, and even though Emily knew that notion was perfectly ridiculous, she still felt as if she'd just overstepped the bounds of good taste.

Tongue in cheek, she apologized for her inexcusable lapse in refinement, then continued as if the baby girl in her arms was just as familiar as she was with the rules of proper etiquette. "Please allow me to introduce myself. I am your neighbor, Emily Hartcourt, and what, pray tell, is your name?"

To her astonishment, her facetious inquiry gained a matter-of-fact response. "Angela Ruth Peddy."

Though she couldn't quite reconcile herself to the fact that she was engaged in a give-and-take conversation with a person who hadn't even been on this earth long enough to grow a full head of hair, Emily's polite reply came out almost by rote. "It's a pleasure to meet you, Angela."

As if by mutual agreement, they both lapsed into silence after that. Angela smiled benignly, seemingly quite content with the outcome of their friendly exchange as they proceeded along the driveway, but Emily's expression became more and more quizzical. Even though she knew next to nothing about young children, she was beginning to suspect that there was something quite unusual about this one.

The growing wet spot on her pleated white cotton skirt confirmed that she was dealing with an extremely immature individual, yet the youngster seemed to possess what Emily felt was an unusually high degree of verbal skills and comprehension. Even so, that suspicion didn't change her view of the present situation and she had every intention of relaying that view to the neglectful parent who had allowed this small, uh . . . baby for lack of a better word, to place herself in such peril. If by some fluke, Angela had managed to place the car into gear, she might have died!

Unfortunately, nobody came in response to the ringing of the chimes, and no matter how hard she pounded on the door, nobody answered the summons. "Your parents must be extremely sound sleepers," Emily declared, yet her irritation with her somnolent new neighbors didn't give her the nerve to barge right into their house, even if they had left their front door unlocked.

"Maybe they'll wake up if they hear you," Emily suggested, as she pushed the door open a crack. "Can you call out for your mommy and daddy, Angela?"

The little girl stared blankly back at her, which made Emily think that she might have overestimated the child's abilities to understand. "Say 'mommy,'" Emily prompted.

Silence.

"How about 'daddy'? Can you say 'daddy'?"

Angela frowned resentfully, then commanded, "You find Daddy! Now!"

Emily considered her frustrating predicament for a moment longer, then decided to enter the house. If anyone questioned her audacity in doing so, she would simply tell them that she was following Angela's orders. As she stepped into the light airy foyer, however, and looked from right to left, Emily stopped dead in her tracks.

Of course she'd been aware that some extensive remodeling had been done to the stately old residence in the months before the new owner had taken possession. The constant parade of trucks and vans had been the talk of her household for weeks. She and her aunts had admired the painstaking efforts that had been made to preserve the home's redbrick exterior, but now that she was seeing some of the interior work firsthand, she couldn't help but feel more than a little envious, especially when she thought about the long list of repairs that needed to be done at Hartcourt House.

Compared to this house, hers would be deemed a mansion, but now she had visual proof that bigger didn't necessarily mean better. Compared to this marvelously updated and beautifully redecorated home, Hartcourt House looked like something that had been designed and furnished back in the Dark Ages. Of course Emily would never dream of saying such a thing to Aunt Esther, who revered every warped floor, stuck window and miswired chandelier in their home, but Emily was still young enough to face a few facts, and the fact was that she coveted her new neighbor's house.

Bypassing the spiral staircase that rose from the center of the cathedral foyer, Emily entered the spacious two-story great room, which she determined was the home's centerpiece. Not that the adjoining sun-filled parlor wasn't lovely, but with its overhead loft, polished hardwood floors and a fireplace surrounded by built-in shelves, the great room was spectacular. The rear wall was all glass, facing a huge deck that overlooked the wooded ravine.

The first floor also contained a cozy study, with wall-to-wall bookshelves; a full bath; and a kitchen with beautiful cherry cabinets and a center island, which held a mind-boggling array of state-of-the-art equipment. The island separated the work area from an informal dining room, which boasted an enormous bay window and a nine-foot ceiling. Emily was so impressed by everything she saw that, left to her own devices, she might have forgotten all about her motive for searching the house, but Angela wouldn't let her forget.

As they walked from room to room, the child sing-songed, "Find Daddy. Find Daddy. Find Daddy."

Eventually, Emily was forced to acknowledge that there was no errant parent to be found on the first floor, which meant that she had to continue the search in the second-floor bedrooms. Horrified by the prospect of barging in on a sleeping couple in their private boudoir, she called up the stairwell, "Hello there! Can anybody hear me? I have your daughter with me."

To her dismay, the only response she got from the second floor was the mild echo of her own voice bouncing off the magnificent cathedral ceiling. "I really wish I didn't have to do this, Angela," she declared grimly as she mounted the stairs. "But what other choice do I have?"

"Find Daddy," Angela directed. Emily rolled her eyes.

Feeling like a reluctant voyeur on her way to a peep show, Emily hesitantly opened the door to the first bedroom at the top of the stairs, but when she saw the undersized furniture, overstuffed toy box and pretty white-and-pink decor, she concluded the room was Angela's. A second, elegantly furnished bedroom proved to be equally unoccupied, which left Emily with only two more options. She cleared her throat very loudly as she continued down the wide hallway and came to a stop in front of the next door. She thought she heard some sort of sound from within, but after waiting for several seconds, the sound wasn't repeated. Taking a deep breath for courage, she pushed open the door and took a hesitant step inside what appeared to be the master suite.

Angela immediately squirmed to be put down on the floor, and soon after, Emily discovered that the child's daddy was indeed waiting for them in his bedroom, though he wasn't there in the flesh. The massive king-size bed, which stood in the center of a distinctly masculine room, hadn't been slept in, but Angela didn't seem the least bit troubled by that disheartening fact as she snatched a five-by-seven frame off the bedside table and turned around to show Emily a picture of a tall blond man holding a newborn baby swaddled in pink blankets.

"My daddy," she announced in smiling satisfaction, but when Emily stepped forward, she hugged the picture to her far-less-than-ample bosom and issued a clear warning. "Hers mine! Not you!"

It was obvious that the child hadn't completely grasped the concept of personal pronouns, but Emily got the general idea. In the brief amount of time she'd been given to study the picture, she'd also managed to recognize the man whom Angela claimed as her own private property, and that recognition not only inspired a great deal of shock but an acerbic reply. "That's just fine with me, young lady. Hers is all yours!"

"My daddy," Angela repeated in a much more conciliatory tone, but Emily wasn't listening. She was still trying to absorb the fact that Angela's name wasn't Peddy at all. It was Petty, and her blond blue-eyed hunk of a father was none other than "Zoomer" Petty, the flamboyant former quarterback of the Columbus Cougars! Upon his retirement last season from professional football he'd become a man who, according to the local sports media, liked to travel in the fast lane, a man who was said to have divorced his boring nonentity of a wife because he preferred to live on a steady diet of glitz, glamour and glory—yet he'd chosen to live in one of the oldest, quietest and most conservative neighborhoods in Ohio's capital city!

"This is incredible!" Emily exclaimed. "I can't even imagine what Aunt Esther's going to say."

For weeks now, she and her aunts had been speculating on the identity of the person who had purchased the old Radford estate. Considering the vast amount of money needed to completely revamp the historic residence, Esther had assumed that the home had been bought by a rich doctor or lawyer. "Only a well-established professional person would make such an effort to preserve the original exterior. Our new neighbor looks to be a man who appreciates history and tradition."

Aunt Ida's guess had been far more disturbing. "Maybe he's a South American drug lord who's establishing a Midwest connection, but wants to appear like a law-abiding citizen. If that's the case, then we'll have strange men coming and going all night. Strange men armed with illegal weapons and driving black unmarked sedans."

Since the fanciful seventy-year-old woman had been having trouble sleeping ever since that possibility had occurred to her, Emily couldn't wait to tell her that there was no need to establish a neighborhood crime watch. Some people might view the star quarterback as a thief who had held up the owner of the Columbus Cougars for an insane amount of money in exchange for his playing football for one extra year, but Emily was reasonably certain that Aunt Ida didn't need to hide the good silver.

It was obvious that Zoomer Petty had retired with enough money to burn, though that knowledge only increased Emily's disdain for him. Just because of his expert ability to throw a football around, this man could afford to pay for anything he wanted, while she, a woman who had earned three advanced degrees in liberal arts, had to worry over every single expenditure.

Unlike Ida, who was an avid Cougar fan, Emily considered football a mindless brutal game of no redeeming value, and she couldn't comprehend why athletes with dim-witted names like Snake, Mad Dog and Zoomer commanded such outrageous salaries. It was also totally beyond her comprehension how such a one-dimensional person could produce such an advanced child, a thought that reminded her she was still faced with a pressing problem.

"Where else could your daddy be, Angela?" she inquired. "He's not downstairs, and he's not in his bed, so do you know where he is?"

"He's urp," Angela replied. "But I's getting a present."

Emily tried to interpret that nonsensical response, but couldn't imagine what or where "urp" could possibly be. Angela, however, didn't have the patience to stand around and wait for Emily to figure it out. Still clutching the picture to her chest, she toddled out of the room and headed toward a door at the end of the hall.

Since no decent person would leave a small child alone in a house, Emily assured that Angela knew exactly where she was going. She just wished that the toddler had taken her there sooner. Now that she knew her neighbor's identity, Emily couldn't wait to get a confrontation with him over with, tell him a few things about a father's responsibility to keep his child safe.

"Mr. Petty?" Emily called, as she followed Angela down the hall. "Mr. Petty? Are you up here? I have your daughter, Angela, with me. I found her outside in your car about to drive away."

For the first time since entering the house, Emily received a response from the other side of a closed door, though it wasn't anything like the one she expected. She heard a groan, then a voice that not only came from a woman, but one obviously on the verge of hysteria. "Oh, thank God!" the voice sobbed. "Thank God, she's all right!"

Emily needed no further urging. She pushed open the door, then hurried forward when she saw a stout middle-aged woman lying on the floor next to an overturned wooden chair. Even though it was clear the woman was in so much pain she found it difficult to talk, the instant she saw Emily, a rush of words came tumbling out. "I never should have gotten up on that chair, but it was still dark outside when we woke up this morning and the light bulb in my room had burned out. I was trying to change it when I lost my balance."

Emily knelt down and clasped the woman's hand in her own, trying to convey some sort of reassurance, but before she could ask where it hurt, the woman exclaimed, "It's my hip! The pain's so bad I...I couldn't make it to the phone. I told Angela to bring the phone to me, but the cord wouldn't stretch far enough, so bless her little heart, she...she tried to dial the thing herself, but she's only two. I tried to stop her from leaving the room, but then I...I guess I must have fainted. I was just starting to come around when I heard your voice."

She immediately started sobbing again. "Thank God you found her. If anything had happened to her, I never would've forgiven myself. Never!"

Angela, who had plopped her soggy backside down on the floor, patted the woman's shoulder, shaking her head sadly as she gazed up at Emily. "Marnie gots a big owie and gots to go to the doctor."

"Yes, she does," Emily replied briskly, then stood up, deciding that all further conversation could wait until she'd called for an ambulance. It took only a few seconds for her to locate the phone and give the correct information to the 911 operator. Then she returned to the injured woman, whom she suspected might be going into shock, quickly covered her with a blanket that she'd pulled off the bed and assured her that everything was going to be all right.

"I wish I could do something to make you more comfortable before the ambulance arrives, but they don't want you to move a muscle until they evaluate your condition," she said as she knelt back down on the floor and reclaimed the woman's hand. "In the meantime, Marnie, you're not to worry. Okay? I'm here now, and I'm going to take care of everything that needs taking care of. I promise."

Three hours later, Emily returned from the hospital with a detailed understanding of what that promise actually entailed. No less mind-boggling was the prospect of explaining those details to her aunts, but after the rather hurried phone call she'd made to them from the emergency room, she knew they would pounce on her the moment she entered the door. Ready or not, that moment was now upon her.

"Don't be scared, Angela," she advised the little girl in her arms. "Aunt Esther's bark is much worse than her bite."

"Doggie says woof, woof, woof," Angela barked noisily as Emily struggled to push open the front door without dropping the bouncing child or the heavy diaper bag that was slipping lower and lower on her left arm. Before she managed to complete the task, however, the door was pulled open from the other side, and she and Angela were faced with her two wild-eyed female relatives.

As was her way, Esther gazed down at them from her imposing height in matriarchal silence, using her gray eyes to convey her disapproval and horror at Emily's frazzled appearance, while Ida bustled about the dim foyer like a short ruffled brown hen. "My goodness, Emily, you're a sight, and this poor, poor little dear. My, my, my," she lamented dramatically, wringing her soft hands together in agitation as Emily stumbled forward into the house. "Left all alone in the care of strangers."

"Believe me, Aunt Ida," Emily warned, deliberately avoiding Aunt Esther's censorious gaze as she dropped the diaper bag on the frayed Aubusson carpet and readjusted Angela on her hip. "This young lady doesn't consider anybody a stranger."

"What on earth is that child trying to say?" Esther demanded, her steel-gray brows arched so high on her forehead that they almost formed a perfect M. "And why must she say it at such a rude volume? None of us is deaf!"

To Emily's amusement and to the astonishment of her two aunts, Angela didn't require anyone to answer for her. "That's what the doggie says!" she insisted with a disdainful shake of her small head, as if she couldn't believe someone, especially an adult, would be stupid enough not to recognize the familiar sound. "Doggie says woof, woof, woof!"

"My stars!" Esther exclaimed.

"Not afraid to speak her mind, is she?" Ida observed.

"And that's not even the half of it," Emily declared, deciding there was no time like the present to announce, "She'll be staying with us until Monday when her father returns from urp, er, Europe."

It took several moments for Esther to recover her aplomb, but then she stepped forward with the take-charge manner that had been developed and honed over three-quarters of a century. "I am most anxious to hear how you managed to get us into this predicament, Emily Anne, but it is quite obvious to me that we shan't manage to exchange a word until this outspoken child is properly settled. I suggest that Ida take her into the kitchen while you and I discuss the matter."

Under different circumstances, Emily might have protested, especially since the phrase "properly settled" ignited a spark of resentment inside her that she hadn't felt so profoundly since she'd been a small rambunctious child herself. She was taken aback by the strength of that feeling, but was wise enough not to act on it. Once Esther had been apprised of the entire story, Emily knew she was going to be twice as upset as she was now, and a "properly settled" young woman like herself understood that the best way to weather the upcoming storm was to remain calm.

Five minutes later, she and Aunt Esther were seated across from one another in the front parlor and Emily was relaying the precipitous events leading up to the arrival of their precocious houseguest. "What did you say the nanny's name was?" Esther inquired after listening to her niece describe the lengthy hospitalization and recovery period required for a broken hip.

"Margaret Hendricks," Emily supplied. "Angela calls her Marnie."

"And are you quite certain that Miss Hendricks said there are no other relatives we might call?"

"Except for the paternal grandparents, who live in California, Angela has nobody but her father, and he has business obligations that will keep him in London for another four days."

Esther's expression was thoughtful. "Zachary Petty... Petty. That name sounds so familiar."

Since Aunt Ida had spent every Sunday afternoon during football season for the past eight years expounding on the talents of the Cougars' star quarterback, Emily knew why the name sounded familiar, but

Esther was focusing her memory on a far more distant past. "Perhaps he's some relation to the Cincinnati Pettys, who made their fortune in banking. I haven't heard mention of the family for the past several decades, but when Grandfather James was alive, I believe he conducted a great deal of business through their bank. If our new neighbor is any relation to them, of course, we must do our very best by his daughter."

Upon hearing that, Emily would have given her eyeteeth to establish some kind of connection between the Cincinnati Pettys and the man next door, but if there was one, she didn't know about it and Aunt Esther was a stickler for the truth. Therefore, she took a deep breath and dropped the bombshell she'd been carrying around all morning. "Angela's father is Zoomer Petty, Aunt Esther. The professional quarterback? And he's in London to participate in an all-star exhibition football game. Supposedly, the event has been sold out for months because it's been publicized as the great Zoomer Petty's last hurrah on the playing field."

The stunned look on her aunt's face was comical, but Emily didn't dare laugh. "He's only going to be gone for four more days," she murmured soothingly when she saw that the older woman's jaw was working but no words were coming out. "And no matter who the man is, as his closest neighbors, we still have an obligation to help."

Esther lifted her chin at this unsubtle reminder of her own convictions, though the expression in her eyes revealed her shock that such a humanitarian philosophy would one day come back to haunt her. "You're quite right, of course, my dear."

Then, just in case her niece had forgotten another oft-repeated tenet, she decreed autocratically, "In the case of an emergency, we Hartcourts can always be relied upon to rise to the challenge, whether the call comes from our nation, our city, our church or some...some..."

Emily supplied a few of the unpalatable labels her aunt was probably searching for. "Gamester? Athlete? Weekend warrior?"

"Indeed," Esther declared with a shudder, lifting her eyes heavenward as if seeking spiritual strength. "Indeed."

Assuming she'd just attained the only semblance of permission she was ever likely to receive, Emily got up from her chair and started for the kitchen. "I'll go place the call to him as soon as I check on Angela. Between the three of us, I'm sure we'll be able to manage her, but Marnie warned me that she's a bundle of energy."

"Emily!"

Wincing at the shrill note in her aunt's voice, Emily stopped, but when she turned back around, her expression was carefully blank. "Yes, Aunt Esther?"

"Call the man collect!"

Two

Looking like a woman who had just triumphed over impossible odds, Ida rushed into the parlor and announced, "Mission accomplished. Angela's sound asleep in that portable crib you brought over."

Esther lifted her eyes toward the heavens and praised a merciful Lord while Emily clasped one hand over her heart and slumped back on the couch. "It's a miracle," she sighed, but a second later, she furrowed her brow. "You're absolutely sure she's asleep this time, Aunt Ida? You're positive she's not faking again?"

"When I left your room she was snoring," Ida said smugly.

A declaration of world peace couldn't have garnered a more heartfelt response. "Snoring," Esther repeated in a rapturous tone, raising a trembling blue-veined hand to her head to push up the bun, which for the first time in recent memory, was sagging down toward her left ear. "The child is snoring."

For the next several moments all three women basked in the delightful silence produced by Aunt Ida's success, but eventually, even though six hours in young Angela's disruptive company had almost depleted her of the energy to lift a finger, Emily remembered a task that couldn't be put off any longer.

"I guess I'd better put through another phone call to her father," she murmured without enthusiasm. "Surely the man's back in his hotel room by now."

"Humph," Esther sniffed. "It's no surprise to me that you've had trouble reaching him. I've read about some of those football players. They've been known to throw wild parties in their hotels and gad about with shameful floozies into the wee hours."

Ida glanced down at the cameo watch pinned to her chocolate-stained bosom, her brows lifting in surprise when she saw how much time had elapsed since she'd last recorded the hour. "My goodness, Emily! Do you realize that it's nearly four in the morning over there?"

"It is?" Emily replied incredulously, but after exchanging a meaningful glance with Aunt Esther, the corners of her lips turned upward in an implacable smile. "Why, so it is," she pronounced in satisfaction as she forced her weary bones to rise from the couch and make the short walk down the hall to the phone in the library.

Sinking gracefully into the plush brown leather chair behind her great-grandfather James's rolltop desk,

Emily picked up the receiver and for the fifth time that day dialed the series of numbers Margaret Hendricks had written down for her. As she listened to the rhythmic clicks that signaled the transmission of her trans-Atlantic call, she thought about Aunt Esther's low opinion of football players, and she lapsed into her lifelong habit of daydreaming, entertaining herself with the mental picture of a certain famous quarterback who had just returned to his room after a wild all-night party.

Hung over and exhausted, the man would collapse atop the satin sheets in his exclusive European hotel, completely oblivious to the come-hither antics of some scantily clad "floozy" who was hoping to share his bed. The woman would leave in a huff because he was snoring like a band saw, but he'd be immersed in some erotic dream, completely unaware that his brief solitude was about to be shattered by the jarring ring of a phone.

At first it would be difficult for him to understand that the intrusive sound wasn't part of the enjoyable fantasy he was having and it would take a while for him to rouse himself out of his alcohol-induced slumber, but then he would lift one hand to grope for the phone on the nightstand, possibly knocking a vase onto the floor, an expensive Chinese vase that the hotel management would demand he replace, then—

"What!"

Caught up in her reverie, Emily was nearly startled out of her wits when a gruff demanding voice answered her call on the very first ring. "Uh...uh, is this

Mr. Petty?'' she asked hesitantly once she'd recovered the use of her voice. "Mr. Zachary Petty?''

Several seconds of silence followed her inquiry, but then a deep rumbling demand sounded in her ear. "Yeah, this is Zack Petty. Now who the hell are you, lady, and why in the devil would you be rude enough to call me at this ungodly hour?''

Considering the number of hours that she and her aunts had labored over Angela on his behalf, Emily had expected to feel a perverse pleasure in disturbing this man's rest, but instead, she was the one who felt disturbed. There was something about the husky caliber of his voice that did very troubling things to her insides, and the suppressed rage in his tone also made her extremely nervous.

To make matters worse, when Emily was nervous, she had the dickens of a time forming a simple sentence. "Well...I...uh...I'm Emily Hartcourt, and I'm calling about your little...uh, girl.''

"Angela!" he practically shouted into the phone. "You're calling about my daughter? Has something happened to her?''

"Well...in a matter of speaking...I suppose one could say that...uh...''

"What?" he commanded, quick to lose patience. "Dammit woman! Say what?''

It had never been her intention to frighten the man, but realizing that she was responsible for the touch of panic she heard in his voice, Emily hurried to explain the reason for her unwelcome phone call. As she launched into the incredible tale of how she'd come to have his daughter in her care, she knew she was stammering, but she couldn't seem to help herself. Her words fell all over themselves as she told him about Angela's attempt to drive his car and her arrival on the scene, and then, instead of continuing the explanation in a straightforward manner the way any normal person would, she offered him a highly unnecessary apology for her unlawful entry into his house. By the time she ended her halting speech with the hospital's prognosis for Miss Hendricks and her broken hip, she feared that she'd come off sounding like a blithering half-wit.

It was clear that Zachary Petty had arrived at a similar conclusion, for Emily detected a definite note of horror in his voice when he demanded, "You're not that little old—the woman who putters around all day in that garden on the other side of my hedge?"

Emily winced at his question. She had warned Aunt Ida that their new neighbors would notice her attempts to spy on them through the privacy hedge, but for some reason, the elderly woman had refused to believe that anyone would be able to discern much difference between her distinctive blue hair and the spirea's dark green foliage.

"Actually I'm her niece," Emily replied weakly, but to her dismay, that admittance didn't inspire any additional confidence on Zachary's part.

"So you're the younger one?"

"Yes," Emily replied, affronted by her suspicion that this man wasn't thinking in terms of decades when he estimated the difference in ages between herself and her aunts.

"The woman who gets up at the crack of dawn every morning to sweep the front sidewalk?"

His poor judgment concerning her age was insulting, but hearing that she'd also been deemed only slightly less dotty than her elderly aunt made Emily bristle, and the spurt of temper she felt eased the nervous flutters in her stomach. Whatever this annoying man thought, her activities were not the least bit strange, and she intended to tell him so in no uncertain terms. "Perhaps if you were widely traveled, Mr. Petty, or cognizant of our family's Danish heritage, you wouldn't consider sweeping our walk such an odd custom," she informed him haughtily. "That daily chore is embraced by the populations of many European countries, especially those of the Netherlands."

Proving that he was more well-read than she'd assumed any professional athlete would be, even though his response was hateful and crude, Zachary retorted, "Don't tell me you folks are still throwing slop out the windows! Haven't you people heard of modern plumbing?"

Emily refused to grace his indelicate question with an answer, allowing her silence to speak for her, but then she recalled that, despite Aunt Esther's feelings on the matter, she was the one paying for this phone call, which meant she couldn't afford to wait around for her point to sink in. Undoubtedly, considering whom she was talking to, any attempt she made to censure his coarseness would fall on deaf ears.

Using the voice she normally reserved for her more smart-alecky students, she suggested, "Perhaps, Mr.

Petty, this conversation would be better served if we set such petty matters aside and limited our discussion to the arrangements that must be made for Angela due to your untimely absence.''

As expected, a man of his questionable mental abilities needed a few moments to comprehend her meaning, but eventually he agreed with her frigidly polite suggestion. ''You're right there, Miss Hartcourt. My concern is for Angela, and believe me, if there was any way I could arrange it, I'd be on the next plane to Columbus!''

Once again, Emily sensed an underlying insult in his words, and her reply was uncharacteristically spiteful. ''But of course your football game must come first.''

Her accusation was followed by a long deadly silence, the same kind of silence she'd just used to put him in his place. However, like the last nerve-racking pause in their conversation, she was the first one to break under the pressure. Only this time, Emily was forced to admit that her long-distance phone bill had nothing to do with her decision. Incredibly, a man who answered to the name of ''Zoomer'' possessed the knack for making her feel extremely uncomfortable. ''Uh, forgive me, Mr. Petty. Perhaps, I . . . I shouldn't have passed judgment on you without knowing more of the facts.''

''Then let me share a few facts with you, Miss Hartcourt.''

''By all means,'' she allowed virtuously.

As he went on to explain the complicated terms under which he'd agreed to play in the all-star game,

Emily could hear the frustration and anxiety in his voice—which at least proved one thing. The boorish man did have his head in the proper place where his young daughter was concerned. After listening to his detailed explanation of publicity contracts and professional loyalties, she assured him that there was no need for him to fly right home.

Unfortunately, in order to allay his fears about her ability to care for Angela, she practically had to tell him her entire life story. Of course, she resented having to play "twenty questions" with a total stranger, but at the same time, she knew that if Angela had been her child, she would've demanded the same kind of information.

After what seemed an eternity, he seemed satisfied with her answers, but it didn't make her too happy to realize that her description of herself had not only convinced him that she was qualified to look after his precious daughter, but had also reinforced the idea that she was a harmless middle-aged spinster, a kind-hearted history professor who spent most of the year confined to a stuffy college classroom. Still, she could hardly fault him for embracing that opinion. His less than complimentary assumptions about her had been based on the damning statements that had come out of her very own mouth.

Even so, there was a noticeably sharp edge to her voice when she brought their depressing conversation to a close. "Then I'll expect to see you on Monday afternoon, Mr. Petty."

"Yes," he agreed. "And I'll call you every day to check up on my baby. I know she looks like butter won't melt in her mouth, but my little Angel can be quite a handful when she wants to be."

Actually his precious "Angel" was much more than a handful whether or not she was trying, Emily amended silently to herself, but instead of voicing that opinion, she said, "Of course, if it would make you feel better to call, feel free."

"Around noon?"

"Noon will be fine. Goodbye until then, Mr. Petty."

"Goodbye."

The receiver was almost back in its cradle when she heard him shout, "Emily! Emily, don't hang up!"

Still nursing her wounded vanity, she was tempted to ignore him, but the sound of her first name on his lips astonished her so much that she lifted the phone back to her ear. "Yes, I'm still here."

"Will you kiss my daughter for me, Emily? Kiss her and tell her I love her very, very much."

That sensually disturbing caliber was back in his deep husky voice, and putting that together with the picture she had of him speaking to her while reclining in bed, Emily swallowed hard. For the first time in several years, she wondered if any man would ever express such sweet and tender feelings in regard to her, of if she was doomed to live a solitary life in an all-female household. "I'll tell her, Mr. Petty," she promised softly. "I'll give her a kiss for you and tell her that you love her the instant she wakes up."

Unfortunately that instant arrived far sooner than Emily had hoped. Angela was raring to go again as soon as the sun came up, uncaring that in order to function at her normal capacity, Emily required another full hour of sleep. Still, less than thirty minutes after crawling out of bed, Emily had reason to be grateful that Angela was such an early riser. If the child hadn't gotten her up when she had, she wouldn't have been fully dressed when the doorbell rang.

Emily settled a bright-eyed and bushy-tailed Angela on her right hip and slowly descended the stairs.

"Now, who the hell could that be?" she mimicked silently under her breath, delighted with herself for not faltering over the word *hell*. "And why the devil would anyone be rude enough to call upon me at this ungodly hour?"

Hoping her expression revealed her dark mood, Emily pulled open the door, but as soon as she got a glimpse of their unexpected caller, her brown eyes widened incredulously and her mouth fell open.

Standing on the step was a black man taller and broader than she had ever seen in her life. His mass was daunting enough, but he was dressed in a garish pink polka-dot shirt, plaid shorts and a pair of purple athletic shoes in a size so large it boggled the imagination. And his head! It was totally bald on one side and the hair on the other side was carved into a bizarre kind of design.

Nonplussed, Emily simply stood there and stared up at the man, but Angela didn't suffer a similar reaction. She held out her arms to him and squealed joyously, "Boom Boom! My Boom Boom!"

"Yo!" the man replied, and grinned hugely.

An hour later, as Emily sat in the breakfast nook watching Angela poking all ten of her fingers into a tub of soft margarine, she still hadn't recovered completely from her startling encounter with Brian "Boom Boom" Taylor. Although the man had made several attempts to explain it to her, she still wasn't exactly certain what position a "nose tackle" played on a football team. Even so, considering his massive bulk, she thought it quite likely Mr. Taylor was an excellent choice for the job. If she'd been a member of an opposing team and come face-to-face with the imposing man during a game, she would've immediately turned tail and run.

Unfortunately that opportunity had been denied her this morning. Like a tiny guided missile, Angela had launched herself off Emily's hip and into the giant's arms before Emily could stop her. Then, with her arms wrapped tightly around what had to be a fifty-inch neck, the child had blithely invited him into the house, and the genial hulk had promptly accepted. To make matters worse, once inside, the man had proceeded to question Emily as if he were the Grand Inquisitor and she a possible heretic. Thoroughly intimidated by his size and suspicious demeanor, Emily had answered every single question, even those that had definitely bordered on the rude.

After the initial shock of the encounter had worn off, Emily realized that Zachary Petty had sicced the giant on her in order to double-check the story she'd given him over the phone, but that knowledge didn't do much to soothe her ruffled feathers. "So he'll tell your dad that I look solid and dependable, will he?" she muttered darkly to Angela. "As if my looks should have anything to do with my ability to take care of you! Now that's the kind of sexist assumption that really makes me angry!''

Angela cocked her head to one side and stared solemnly back at her. Assuming the annoyance in Emily's voice was directed at her, she lifted her goopy hand out of the margarine container, wiped her fingers down the front of her clean yellow smock and inquired unrepentantly, "All done?"

"All done," Emily agreed wryly, but she greatly feared that where Angela was concerned they were only just starting.

And over the next three days, Emily discovered that she was right to be afraid. As any good neighbor would do, she'd devoted herself to the child, but in the process she'd gained a thorough understanding of why some species of animals chose to eat their own young. Unless she was sleeping, an inactive state that the toddler tried to avoid for as long as was humanly possible, Angel, as her misguided father called her, was constantly in flight. Unable to anticipate the child's constant takeoffs and ill-placed landings, Emily and her aunts wished that they had been born with ten hands and several pairs of eyes in the back of their heads. Perhaps if they had been, they could've prevented a bit more of the youngster's happy destruction of their personal property, or even more importantly, foreseen her uncanny talent for wrapping all three of them around her busy little finger.

To Emily's amazement, by the time Zoomer Petty was scheduled to return home, Aunt Ida was predicting that the obviously gifted little girl would grow up to be a female Albert Einstein. Even Aunt Esther, who had obviously mellowed considerably over the years, was admitting that the mischievous imp possessed a fair amount of charm.

As for Emily, because of the affection she had developed for the child, she'd begun to think a bit more charitably toward the father. After all, she conceded, the man might be tactless and overbearing, but to have produced such an amazing offspring he had to possess some degree of intelligence. Adding even more to his credit was the fact that he had kept his promise and called to check up on Angela every single day.

Emily continued to believe that Zachary Petty might be a decent sort of man when Monday afternoon arrived and she witnessed his joyful reunion with his daughter. As soon as Aunt Ida opened the front door and Angela saw Daddy standing outside, the child dashed across the foyer as fast as her little legs would carry her and threw herself into her smiling father's waiting arms.

"Hi, poppet. Looks like you missed me as much as I missed you," Zachary exclaimed with a laugh as he scooped her up. The two of them hugged as if it had been months instead of days since they'd last seen each other.

Like Aunt Esther, Emily paused in the entryway to the parlor in order to give father and daughter a few moments of privacy, but politeness wasn't her only reason for hanging back. She'd known that this man was good-looking by that photo she'd seen of him in his bedroom, and the pictures she'd seen of him in the newspapers had shown him to be in great physical shape, but Zoomer Petty in the flesh was an entirely different story. None of those pictures had done justice to his ruthlessly handsome features, or his hair, which was not just blond, but a rich tawny gold, streaked with silver. And his eyes reminded her of the polished brilliance of aquamarines, not quite blue, not quite green, but crystal clear as the sea and startlingly beautiful against his tanned skin.

Then there was his body. Lordy! Even without the added stature of shoulder pads, she could tell he possessed a fabulous physique. Tall and broad-shouldered, he also had the trim waist, narrow hips and muscled thighs that had the power to change a simple pair of faded jeans into a sexy advertisement for whatever designer label he happened to be wearing.

What was more, Emily had the utterly shameful urge to ask him to turn around so she could check out the part of his anatomy that would sport such a label, and the urgency of that need embarrassed her so badly that the blood rushed to her face. Naturally that *would* be the exact moment he chose to look at her, and as if finding those gorgeous eyes on her wasn't disconcerting enough, he greeted her with a brilliant smile, as though they were long-lost friends.

"It's great to see you, Emily, and I can't thank you enough for coming to the rescue of my family. I spoke to Marnie this morning and she told me how efficiently you took charge after her accident. I know I've already said so on the phone, but I want to tell you again how much I appreciate your kindness toward her and my daughter. You've been a real lifesaver to all three of us."

As she had the first time she'd spoken to him on the phone, Emily stammered around for something suitable to say, upset with herself for being utterly unnerved by his physical presence and completely rattled by his compliments. She mumbled some inane response, which made her feel foolish, and Zachary smiled indulgently at her, which made her feel even worse.

"I would also like to thank your aunts," Zack said, turning to face Aunt Esther, who wasn't the least bit nervous in the presence of such a blatantly virile young man, nor impressed by the fact that he was a legendary figure on the gridiron. After introducing herself and Aunt Ida to him, she invited imperiously, "Do come inside, Mr. Petty, and tell us more about yourself."

Aunt Ida wasn't shy, either. She promptly backed up Esther's invitation with a heartfelt request for a play-by-play description of the all-star game. "I especially want to hear about that sneaky trap play in the first quarter. Did you call that in the huddle or did Coach Williams send it in from the sidelines?"

Sandwiched between the two elderly women, Zachary Petty was ushered firmly toward the parlor, but before passing through the wide archway he stopped and shot Emily a questioning look. "Aren't you coming?" he inquired in a tone that sounded slightly desperate, and Emily couldn't prevent herself from smiling at how her aunts could overwhelm a man like him.

"After I prepare some refreshments," she replied sweetly, thankful to see that her voice was functioning quite normally again and so was her brain. That being the case, she couldn't think of a more perfect time to let him know how much she'd appreciated the frequent unscheduled visits of one snoopy mistrustful nose tackle.

"Boom Boom Taylor told me how much you like lemon chiffon pie, so I suggested that Aunt Ida bake one for your homecoming," she told him. "She made it from scratch and she can't wait for you to taste it."

Zachary's brows rose in astonishment, then narrowed speculatively on her face. He had hated lemon chiffon pie ever since training camp of his rookie year when, in the locker room after practice, Boom Boom Taylor and his front-line cronies had held him down and plastered his face with a pie for each time he'd missed a snap from center. If the big man had told Emily that story, then the woman was well aware that the very thought of lemon chiffon still made him want to gag.

Unfortunately he was too much of a gentleman to hurt the feelings of a little old lady, and evidently Emily Hartcourt was counting on that. "I gather that Boom Boom dropped in to see you more than once while I was gone?"

"Actually he dropped by to see us quite frequently," Emily informed him evenly. "At least once or twice a day."

For the first time since meeting her, Zachary realized that there might be much more to this woman than what met the eye. And speaking of eyes, he discovered that hers were not only the color of his favorite brandy, but also contained an impish sparkle that totally amazed him. Suddenly he realized that Miss Emily Hartcourt wasn't the middle-aged nonentity he'd previously judged her to be. In fact, she was not only close to him in age, but very pretty in an elegant understated kind of way, and much brighter than he'd given her credit for.

Actually she was a great deal brighter, Zack admitted, for her choice of vengeance was downright diabolical. "Boom Boom can be slightly overeager at times," he offered hopefully, praying that the woman was also perceptive enough to recognize an apology when she heard one.

"And inquisitive, too," Emily replied, never altering her smooth expression, though the challenging sparkle in those big brown eyes of hers told him that no excuse could justify what she'd been put through by his faithful watchdog. "Why, that man asks almost as many questions as Angela."

Admitting defeat, Zack sighed in resignation, then hiked his beaming daughter higher up on his shoulder and allowed himself to be led away into the parlor. Paybacks were hell, he decided as he smiled politely at the regal-looking elderly woman who ordered him into a chair, but he was a man who prided himself on honoring his debts, and he owed Emily Hartcourt a big one. What she didn't realize, however, was that unlike the herd of women who'd tried to attract his attention in the three years since his divorce had become final, she'd pricked his interest on several different levels today. Once he'd evened the score between them by eating a fair portion of humble pie, he intended to satisfy that curiosity.

Three

***

Zack located his pajama-clad daughter's beloved "blankie" under her bed and offered it beseechingly to her. Angela pretended to be blind. "Tellya what, Daddy," she exclaimed brightly as if about to disclose some fascinating secret. "My Em says I's a pip."

"She's got that right," Zack replied, raking a weary hand through his hair as he slumped back down on the child-size mattress.

Angela rolled over onto her tummy, propped her head on her chubby fists and frowned over at him. "You're wearing your mean face at me," she observed sadly, then scrambled quickly under the pink floral sheet and popped her pacifier back into her mouth. "Tat's bab!"

"Very bad," Zack agreed. "But that's how I feel when my very tired little girl refuses to go to sleep."

Aware that her father was nearing the end of his rope, Angela squeezed her eyes tightly shut, then pulled the plug out of her mouth and offered sweetly, "Night-night, Daddy. Don't bite the bedbugs."

There were times, Zack decided several minutes later, when his baby girl was entirely too smart for her own good, but tonight wasn't one of those times. Even after doing his damnedest to explain jet lag to her, he hadn't been able to convey the debilitating effects of too many time changes combined with not enough sleep. Oblivious to his bloodshot eyes and frequent yawns, she'd felt obliged to fill him in on every exciting detail of her life that he'd missed out on while away. Before he'd finally managed to get his message across, he'd heard about every meal she'd eaten, every "I-don't-need-a-nap" the Hartcourt women had persuaded her to take and each and every interesting object she'd accidently broken during her thrilling exploration of their house.

Following a conversation that was spoken from behind a pacifier wasn't easy, but somewhere in that garbled mishmash, he'd also discovered that a woman named Emily, or as Angel called her, "My Em," had somehow managed to land a spot very high up on his daughter's list of favorite people. Since that accomplishment was reserved for a very small company, only one of whom was female, Zack was almost certain that he'd found the solution to his upcoming child-care problem. As young as she was, Angela's instincts about people were rarely wrong, and every other sentence the child had uttered since he'd come home had begun with, "My Em this or my Em that."

As he descended the stairs to apologize to that patient lady for his keeping her waiting so long, Zack swallowed the aftertaste of lemons and chuckled. No matter how his young daughter felt about Miss Emily Hartcourt, he had reason to believe that the woman wasn't a saint all the time. Beneath that deceptively sweet, astonishingly old-fashioned demeanor, Emily possessed a healthy dose of tart, and Zack had the indigestion to prove it.

Oddly enough, instead of motivating him to sever all further connections with her, the mean-spirited stunt she'd pulled on him with the pie made him think that there was still some hope left for the woman. Of course, after that grilling those elderly aunts of hers had subjected him to this afternoon, he didn't care to run into those two again any time soon, but he still wanted to know more about their mysterious niece, discover if she was hiding any other tantalizing surprises behind that shy, old-world exterior of hers. He also wondered how such an emotionally constrained lady would react if she knew that, except for lemons, he'd always preferred the taste of tart fruits over the sweet ones and that his taste in women ran pretty much along the same lines.

When he reached the bottom step, Zack glanced across the foyer into the great room, shaking his head incredulously when he saw that Emily was still seated on the couch in the exact same position as he'd left her. Obviously uncomfortable in these alien surroundings, she was worrying the hem of her pristine skirt with her fingers, unaware she was revealing a fair amount of leg in the process, an astonishingly shapely leg.

Any man would've heartily enjoyed the view he was being afforded, and Zack knew a host of women who would've been pleased by his admiration, but Emily wasn't aware of his interest in her pretty legs. She was staring straight ahead, as if fearing that a visual investigation of his living room would be a shameful breach of good manners. Remembering how many times during their first phone call that she'd dithered around apologizing for her unauthorized entry into his house, Zack realized that was actually how the poor woman thought.

Now that he'd met her autocratic Aunt Esther, Zack knew how she'd come by her quaint approach to the rules of proper etiquette, but like most other people who still moved with the times, Zack didn't put much emphasis on the dictates of Emily Post. On the other hand, he truly had to admire this Emily's perfect posture. He'd never run across a woman who could sit for any length of time without lowering her chin so much as a centimeter, slumping her perfectly squared shoulders or relaxing her spine. Miss Emily Hartcourt, however, was making no concessions to the more modern laid-back attitude. In her high-necked white blouse, starched navy linen skirt and practical shoes, she looked like a throwback to some straitlaced bygone era, a perfect example of ladylike carriage and deportment.

The proud way she carried herself, however, was only one thing on a growing list of things about the woman that intrigued Zack. With those unconsciously beguiling come-hither brown eyes of hers and that haughty standoffish demeanor, which added ten years to her age, she struck him like a puzzle begging to be solved. Considering her estimation of the mental capabilities of professional athletes, he doubted she'd suspect that solving complex puzzles was one of his favorite hobbies.

His smile widened when he remembered some of the unwitting comments she'd made to him over the phone while they'd been discussing what was best for Angela, the condescending attitude she'd revealed without even realizing she was doing so. Finding out that the senseless "brawn versus brain" theory was held by a reasonably young woman had come as an unwelcome surprise to him, but Zack had been forced to deal with that kind of intellectual snobbery for most of his life, and he knew how to turn that superior attitude of hers to his own advantage.

Emily didn't realize what a weapon she'd inadvertently handed him, but he did and he was greatly looking forward to using it. In Zack's estimation, this dear unsophisticated lady was in desperate need of a healthy shaking up, and after seeing those fabulous legs of hers, he wasn't opposed to seeing himself as the ideal candidate for the job. His years in professional football had familiarized him with every possible line that an overconfident jock might say, so he could take on that role with very little effort. And in the process of providing her with a long overdue education regarding the supposedly inferior male of the species, he could learn everything he was curious to learn about one Miss Emily Hartcourt.

"Thanks for waiting," Zack said as he entered the living room, holding back an amused grin when he noticed her startled jump and the haste with which she pulled down the hem of her skirt to cover her exposed knees. "As I'm sure you know by now, Angela refuses to go to sleep until she runs totally out of steam."

Emily quit daydreaming about how it would feel to be held in the arms of the golden blond, taut-muscled hunk, and shot the real version of her romantic fantasy a nervous smile. She prayed that her expression conveyed compassion for his child-rearing problem rather than the pleasure she'd experienced imagining what his large hands would feel like caressing her body, but even though she told herself that such a thing was never likely to happen, that she'd never allow such an intimate situation to develop between herself and a man like Zachary Petty, she still couldn't seem to stop herself from admiring his fabulous physique.

Noting her vigilant gaze, Zack changed his mind about sharing the couch with her. Not wanting to scare her off before achieving what he wanted, he took the wing chair on the opposite side of the glass coffee table. Her relief was almost palpable, and that irritated Zack so much he had to fight down the urge to point out that he wasn't some masher.

Unfortunately what he did say did nothing to reassure her. "I'd like to proposition you, Emily. You're just the kind of woman I'm looking for."

"I beg your pardon!" she squeaked, the shocked expression on her face telling him exactly what she was thinking. This fanciful female was thinking he was suggesting a compromise to her virtue!

Zack was tired and irritable and he promptly lost all patience with her, totally forgetting he was supposed to be such an insensitive dolt he wouldn't comprehend her unspoken insult to his integrity. "Are you for real, lady?" he demanded sarcastically. "Or did you walk in here straight off the pages of some gothic novel?"

That last question captured Emily's attention, mainly because she couldn't quite grasp the fact that a man who raced up and down a football field throwing a pigskin ball around for several months out of the year was in any way cognizant of that genre of romantic literature, which used medieval locales to effect feelings of foreboding. She stared at him in disbelieving silence for several seconds, then lifted her chin in a manner of which any gothic heroine would be proud and inquired indignantly, "Whatever do you mean by that?"

Zack rolled his eyes. "Lord, woman, will you just listen to yourself!"

Emily stared blankly back at him and Zack groaned. "Whatever do you mean, sir!" he mimicked harshly. "Give me a break! No modern woman talks like that. If I didn't know better I'd think you'd been withering away in some ruin of a castle for the past forty years!"

Stung by his cruel accusations and his inability to believe she was years away from menopause, Emily's retort was out before she could stop it. "Thirty years!" she corrected hotly. "I've only been withering away for thirty years!"

Zack wanted to kick himself when he saw the look of horror that came over her face as soon as she realized what she'd just said, and he felt even worse when he saw how embarrassed she was by the kind of conclusions he was certain to draw from such a telling statement. Her cheeks were flaming and her dark eyes were so bright that he feared she might burst out crying any second.

Counting on the risky assumption that along with her tendency to blush at the slightest thing she also possessed a surprisingly touchy temper, he made himself look even more like a jerk in the hope of making her too angry to cry. "Who would've thought it!" he exclaimed, arching his brows incredulously. "If you're only thirty that makes me four years older than you are!"

The tactic worked, but Zack's success didn't come without a painful price. "And who would've thought that a big dumb jock could subtract two-digit numbers in his head?" Emily muttered furiously under her breath, but not so softly that Zack couldn't hear every word and had to bite his tongue to keep from ripping into her again.

Striving for the most guileless expression in his considerable repertoire, he apologized. "I'm sorry. I didn't hear what you said. Would you mind repeating that?"

As expected, Emily wasn't prepared to insult his intelligence quite that openly. "I said that I find your reaction to my real age incredibly rude!" she exclaimed hotly, then immediately lowered her eyes, disclosing a shyness and vulnerability that made Zack wonder if she'd ever been out on a date with a guy. "Do I really look that old and awful?"

Zack didn't think he'd be doing himself or her any favor by shrugging off her pathetic question, but being brutally honest with a woman who didn't appear to have an ounce of self-confidence went against every grain in his body. He was much more familiar with the self-possessed glamorous types, women who took their beauty for granted and knew how to use it to get whatever they wanted from a man. Emily Hartcourt wasn't even aware she was pretty!

After the way he'd just attacked her, Zack knew he'd given her ample reason to doubt it, but he'd been brought up to be a gentleman, and gentlemen didn't abuse defenseless ladies even when they asked for it. "I think it's your stubbornly correct manner of speaking that makes you seem so much older than you actually are, and the dowdy way you dress only adds to the misconception," he admitted gruffly, wishing now that he'd left well enough alone, especially since the way she talked or looked was really none of his concern.

But then, even if it meant he'd lose the chance of hiring her as his sitter, the woman needed to hear the unvarnished truth from somebody, and he would bet his last nickel that neither one of her blue-blooded aunts would ever tell her the score. If she sequestered herself inside that huge old relic of a house, those two would probably like it just fine.

"C'mon Emily, can't you take a chance and let your hair down just a little?" he inquired gently. "School's out for the summer, and with the hot weather we've been having all June, no one would complain if the teacher exchanged her starchy uniform for a halter top and a pair of shorts."

Emily could name at least one person who would do that very thing, but it suddenly dawned on her that adhering so rigidly to Aunt Esther's decidedly old-fashioned standards made her appear like a woman with no mind of her own. And that just wasn't true! She'd gone along with the program because it made her daily life much easier, but it was clear that Zachary Petty didn't see it that way, which made her wonder if other people had also misjudged her character, saw her as some kind of a wimp. The thought was totally appalling!

To reassure herself that such a misconception wasn't possible, Emily tried to come up with a logical argument to defend her dowdy appearance, but she couldn't think of a single thing to say that would make any sense to him. She was still searching for some scathing retort when he demanded to know if she even owned a pair of shorts. This brought her head up in a flash.

"Of course I do!"

"But you never wear them for fear of offending that curmudgeon of an aunt," Zack suggested knowingly, then took the edge off his accusation by conceding, "I realize that getting along with that snooty old matriarch would try anyone's courage. I'm twice that old biddy's size, but when Esther plunked me down on that hard-backed chair and started firing all those questions at my head, all I wanted to do was cut and run.''

"I noticed,'' Emily murmured dryly.

"I noticed you noticed,'' Zack retorted in a reproachful tone, but there was an engaging twinkle in his aquamarine eyes that made her think he was much more amused than annoyed by her defection. "Actually you took a perverse pleasure in watching the hawk-eyed old termagant drag me off for an interrogation. You thought it was poetic justice, now, didn't you?''

Emily was appalled by the tiny giggle that spilled from between her lips before she could call it back, but she'd never heard her Aunt Esther described in such truthful, if derogatory, terms. At first, she was ashamed of herself for finding his outrageous descriptions of the woman funny, but then she glanced over at Zack, saw his answering grin and realized he didn't think badly of her for being amused by his uncomplimentary labels. He appeared to be happy to learn she had at least some sense of humor, and the approving look he was giving her made her think that he no longer considered her a total washout.

"Didn't anyone ever teach you that it's not nice to call people names?'' she inquired in a halfhearted attempt to demonstrate some degree of family loyalty, but it was apparent to both of them that she was still biting back amusement.

"People have tried to teach me lots of things,'' Zack admitted with a careless shrug. "But it's a free country, and what I choose to learn is an entirely different story."

Emily was sure he wasn't referring to the matter of free choice just to reinforce his point that she didn't seem to be aware of the concept, but the point was well taken. When she returned home, Emily planned to think long and hard about the narrow path she'd been walking for the past two decades and attempt to judge whether or not her journey would take her anywhere she truly wanted to go. After spending the past forty-eight hours watching a tiny tot bulldoze her way through any obstacle that blocked her path, Emily had started to wonder if the detours she'd taken along the way in order to please other people were the right ones for herself. Tonight's conversation with Zachary had stirred up even more questions.

Whatever answers she came to, however, were a personal matter, and she didn't require any more input from a man who knew next to nothing about her or how she truly felt about anything. With that conclusion in mind, she deliberately switched the focus of their discussion away from herself. "I've noticed that Angela holds the same view toward education. If she doesn't want to learn something, she not only says so in no uncertain terms, but she all out refuses to learn it."

Zack was happy for the change in subject, especially when his main motive for asking Emily to come over to his house tonight was to find out if she possessed the rare qualities he considered necessary for dealing with a child who would probably always operate outside the mainstream. "Being a teacher, I imagine you found Angel's attitude extremely frustrating.''

Zack was startled by her trill of laughter, but he liked the low husky sound of it and decided she should laugh much more often. He wasn't sure why she was hiding her light under a bushel basket, or how long she'd been getting away with it, but after watching her dark eyes light up like that, he was more determined than ever to be the man who would drag her out of her inhibited shell.

''Aunt Esther was frustrated a few times and even Aunt Ida threw up her hands once or twice,'' Emily conceded honestly. ''But once I realized that Angela marches to a totally different drummer and accepted that about her, I found her do-or-die approach to life truly delightful.''

''You did?''

''Absolutely,'' Emily assured him. ''At two, she knows herself better than most adults ever do and I can't help but admire that in her, even if it can be frustrating to deal with. For example, my attempts at potty training ran straight into a thick wall of undisputable logic. I got her to use the potty once, but afterward she made it clear that she'd only done so as a favor to me, and as far as she was concerned, that satisfied her obligation.''

Since neither he nor Marnie had been able to convince the stubborn tyke that the bathroom was an important part of the house, Zack was thoroughly impressed. ''You actually got her to use the potty! That's terrific!''

"Once. I only got her to use it once," Emily reminded him, then shrugged her slender shoulders and smiled the beguiling smile that Zack found so appealing. "But even if I do say so myself, it was a step in the right direction, especially when one considers who I was up against."

"It was a major achievement, a stunning accomplishment, a colossal feat," Zack corrected with a flourishing wave of one muscular arm. "A bloody miracle!"

Oh, how the mighty have fallen, Emily thought to herself, her brown eyes sparkling with mirth as she imagined what this macho man's ex-teammates would say if they could hear him waxing poetic over the less than earth-shattering news that his daughter had placed her "wee-wee" in the proper depository. Then she frowned, realizing that her erudite colleagues might have a few choice things to say to her, as well, if they'd been privy to her contributions to this ridiculous conversation, and the more she thought about that, the more foolish she felt.

When Zack got through complimenting her for what, in reality, she knew was next to nothing, she tried to steer their talk into a more meaningful philosophical vein. "Isn't it amazing how one small child has the power to reduce two mature adults to the point where making a success of potty training seems like the most important goal one could ever attain?"

Zack nodded, but unlike Emily, he didn't feel foolish at all for admitting that a baby's wants and needs had forced him to view his whole life from an entirely different perspective and make changes accordingly.

"Potty training is important," he agreed, as if they were still discussing some far-reaching essential truth. "But in actuality I think that getting Angela to sleep through the night has been my greatest accomplishment. Sleep deprivation does terrible things to a man's ability to behave rationally. The week before Angela finally gave up demanding a bottle, which every book I read assured me should've taken place much earlier than six months ago, I went on an insane rampage and destroyed every alarm clock in our old apartment."

Not being a parent, Emily had a difficult time relating to his problems, but she knew enough about Angela to suspect that the child wouldn't do anything on the schedule put down as average in the child-care books. Although Emily had no right to voice an opinion, she'd developed a strong affection for Zack's little girl, and she wanted to know if he'd accepted that irrefutable fact about her or if he was still fighting the inevitable.

"The only areas where Angela seems to lag behind other children her age are those that most people would consider the basics," she observed thoughtfully. "It's been several years, but I had to take a course in child development while working on my undergraduate degree, and Angela strikes me as one of those youngsters who does everything in reverse, though she's not doing so by choice."

"No, she's doing it because she wants to drive her poor father nuts," Zack concluded facetiously.

"She's doing it because she's extremely bright," Emily came back promptly. "It's incredible to watch her spout four-syllable words around a pacifier, but not if you realize that she's been robbing Peter to pay Paul. Even a mighty mite like Angela has only so much energy, and by devoting most of hers to the development of speech and intellect, she's delayed the time for giving up the infantile behaviors that provide her with security."

Zack looked at Emily as if she were the most intelligent creature that had ever walked the earth, and Emily felt her cheeks warm with pleasure until he disclosed his real reason for liking her way of thinking. "Exactly!" he expounded, beaming at her. "And understanding that about my daughter brings me back to the topic I invited you over here to discuss. I'm in desperate need of a baby-sitter, and in my opinion, you're the perfect person to look after Angel until Marnie gets back on her feet."

Zack assumed he'd made some headway with her during the past few minutes, but Emily began to squawk again, looking just as appalled as she had during the beginning of their conversation when she'd jumped to the conclusion he had designs on her body.

"Baby-sit! Me? You must be joking!" she exclaimed. "I know next to nothing about young children, but even if I did, I certainly wouldn't hire myself out as a baby-sitter. I already have a career, Mr. Petty, a challenging highly fulfilling career in the field of higher education."

Emily Hartcourt didn't look very fulfilled, but Zack doubted she'd appreciate that observation. Since it was still too soon in their relationship to unsettle her in the ways he'd like to further on down the line, he pointed out evenly, "But you don't teach any classes in the summer, so you've got the free time to do other challenging things."

"Well, yes, but—"

"But what? You've already proved you're great with her, and you've got to admit that keeping up with my Angel is a worthy challenge for anybody," he persisted, then added with a rakish smile that made Emily's heart flip over, "And I wish you'd stop calling me Mr. Petty. Usually my friends and neighbors feel free to call me Zack."

Aware he was amused with her again for being so hilariously prim and proper, Emily could think of several well-chosen names to call him, but to her disgust, she couldn't find the courage to utter a single one. To make matters worse, Zachary Petty had the unnerving ability to read every nuance of her expression and the gall to bring her to task for her unkind thoughts.

"Okay," he acknowledged in an offended tone, his blue eyes focused intensely on her face. "I can see you don't like me well enough yet to call me by my first name, but how you feel about me doesn't change the fact that my daughter needs you desperately, and Angela's feelings are what's important here. She adores you, Emily, and besides Marnie, you're the only woman she's displayed any affection for since her mother died."

Emily's face paled to the color of chalk. "I...I didn't know that your ex-wife was dead. I assumed that with the kind of mon...well, considering who you are, that you'd won custody of Angela in your divorce.''

The last thing Zack wanted to do was discuss his failed marriage or the nasty custody battle that had taken place afterward, especially since none of it mattered anymore. Instead he informed her bluntly, ''Shirley died in a car accident when Angela was nine months old.''

''I'm very sorry,'' Emily replied, not sure her condolences were required under the circumstances, but unable to think of anything more appropriate to say. If she'd had more interest in professional sports, she might have read the sports pages more often and been more current about Zack's personal situation. Of course, rabid fan that she was, Aunt Ida had disclosed to Emily some of the more scandalous aspects to his high-profile divorce, but if Ida had known the tragic aftermath of that breakup, Emily was sure she would've mentioned it. Since her aunt hadn't said a word to her, Emily could only assume that the death of Zack Petty's ex was not a widely known fact.

In that regard, she said, ''I don't remember anything about an accident being mentioned in the press.''

Zack's normally sunny, blue-green gaze turned cold. ''The press lost interest in Shirley as soon as our divorce became final,'' he said bluntly. ''As far as the media was concerned, it was a matter of 'out of sight, out of mind.' The accident got a small write-up on the back page of the sports section. As my ex-wife, you see, Shirley was ex-news.''

''But what about Angela? Even after the divorce, she was still your daughter,'' Emily stated with a perplexed frown, unable to tell from Zack's closed expression whether he'd been pleased or upset by the press's fickleness.

Zack smiled without humor. "Yes, she was, but her mother was the parent who won the custody battle, and her mother was a nobody."

"Not to Angela!" Emily declared indignantly.

"No," Zack verified heavily, casting Emily a meaningful glance. "Not to Angela."

Four

―――

Two days later, Emily stared up at the swirling plaster design on the cracked ceiling of her bedroom and tried to come up with an explanation for her actions that didn't paint her as a total sucker.

"Okay," she conceded after several moments of useless effort. "So I'm a pushover for a good sob story. So what? Just because I agreed to baby-sit for that sneaky devil of a man doesn't mean I'll allow him to walk all over me any time he chooses. Whether he likes it or not, this arrangement of ours is strictly temporary!"

With that resolution firmly in mind, Emily slipped out of bed and padded to the bathroom to take her shower, but afterward, as she sat at her dressing table to apply a pretty new shade of lipstick to her mouth and highlight her cheekbones with a soft dusting of peach-colored blush, she still hadn't finished delivering a pep talk to herself. As difficult as it was for her to believe, she had recently discovered she was just as susceptible to a pair of boyish dimples and a gorgeous set of baby blues as the next woman, but forewarned was forearmed, she reminded herself, and Zack Petty wouldn't find it so easy to manipulate her in the future. He could turn up the controls on that devastating charm of his to full blast, but she would remain impervious.

With deliberate care, she pulled on a pressed pair of khaki walking shorts and a sleeveless white cotton top, then lifted the lid off the shoe box that contained the new pair of sandals she'd purchased yesterday. And Zack Petty had nothing to do with her decision to rejoin the twentieth century, she assured herself. She couldn't care less how he felt about her new image.

If nothing else, her aunts had taught her it was a mistake for a woman to perceive her own identity through the eyes of a man, and all they'd had to do to underscore that point was remind Emily of what had happened to their naive baby sister—her mother. Instead of seeking a higher education and assuring her future, Elaine Hartcourt had pinned all her hopes and dreams on a ne'er-do-well adventurer and run off with him to live on love without the legal benefits of marriage. Upon her death, five years later, she'd left nothing behind to show for herself but a four-year-old child, fathered by a man with no sense and even less money. Unwilling and unable to shoulder the responsibility of raising Emily, Roger Sims had promptly returned his heartbroken little girl to the bosom of his dead lover's family and taken off for parts unknown, never to be seen or heard from again.

From almost the first day after her arrival at Hartcourt House, Emily had been advised that the wisest thing any woman could do for herself was pursue a college degree and attain a career, thus enabling herself to stand on her own. According to Aunt Esther, every woman should establish a career for herself before even contemplating the possibility of marriage, for husbands and children made a woman more dependent, not independent. Indeed, Esther Hartcourt, who'd retired as the first female principal of Windgate Preparatory School, considered herself a living testament to the virtues of remaining single and saw herself as a strong self-reliant woman who could honestly say she needed nothing from anyone.

Recently, however, Emily had come to the realization that she didn't want to end up like Aunt Esther, though she'd done very little to prevent exactly that from happening. Determined not to follow in the footsteps of her naive and foolish mother, she'd taken her aunt's logical-sounding advice very much to heart and concentrated all her efforts on achieving an education and establishing a career. But, she now realized, she'd accomplished that goal to the exclusion of all else. She was a woman fast approaching her prime, yet she had next to no friends her own age and she could count her relationships with the opposite sex on the fingers of one hand.

Of course neither of the old-fashioned women who had raised her would consider their niece a social misfit, but Emily was beginning to see things differently, and what she saw made it imperative for her to institute some immediate changes. Even if Aunt Esther threw a conniption when she saw Emily's bare legs and brightly painted toenails, she was determined to hang tough. As of today, she was turning over a new leaf. No more kowtowing to other people's expectations, no more compromises for the sake of domestic peace. No more wimping out! The old Emily was going into the closet in mothballs, and the new one was going to be a force to behold.

When she glanced into the cheval mirror next to her bureau, however, and saw the wild disarray of brown curls that framed her face, Emily's resolve wavered. Then she remembered a certain someone's comment about letting her hair down, and she forced herself not to march back to her dressing table and reach for the stack of hairpins. In its natural state her hair was always this curly, and Emily reminded herself that no matter how Aunt Esther felt about it, having naturally curly hair was no sin.

"No guts, no glory," Emily cautioned her mealy-mouthed-looking reflection, then turned on her heel and walked purposefully out of her bedroom.

"You're actually thinking of going next door looking like that!" Aunt Esther exclaimed in a scandalized tone, just as Emily had expected her to do the instant she made her appearance in the kitchen. "Don't you think such a casual outfit is inappropriate for a person who's starting a new position?"

"On a hot day like this, I think a pair of shorts are perfectly appropriate," Emily insisted evenly. "And

I'm baby-sitting, Aunt Esther. Somehow, I think chasing a two-year-old around all day negates the need for formal attire."

"Does it also negate the need to pin up your hair properly?" Esther demanded autocratically.

Emily took a deep breath before replying, but her tone was resolute. "I'd say so. After all, I'm not lecturing to an auditorium full of graduate students. I'm going out to play with a little girl."

"A highly rambunctious little girl," Ida put in helpfully as she stepped in front of Emily to pour hot water from the teapot into her sister's empty cup. "If you recall, Esther, Angela never stands still for much longer than three seconds. At the pace that child sets for herself, Emily would lose all the pins in her hair within the first hour, so why should she bother with them in the first place?"

Esther pursed her lips. "Why indeed?" she said sourly, then introduced the subject that Emily knew her aunt considered to be the crux of the matter. "No matter how hard I try, Emily, I cannot understand why you agreed to take on such a thoroughly thankless chore. It's not as if Mr. Petty couldn't afford to hire someone much more qualified than you to look after Angela, and I would've thought you had quite enough to do already this summer without overburdening yourself like this. Or is compiling our family's history for the founding fathers' committee no longer an important priority for you?"

"Oh, don't worry about that, Aunt Esther," Emily assured the woman, but even as she spoke the words, she started edging closer to the back door. "We've still got six months before the committee's deadline, which leaves me with plenty of time to complete all my necessary writing for their anthology."

"And it's not as if anyone would squawk if she left out a few of the more boring details," Ida said, gesturing with one hand behind her back for Emily to get out of the house while the getting was still good. "Like those meticulous records Grandfather James kept, pertaining to the question of horse feed. I for one, couldn't care less if it turns out that the benefits of linseed meal greatly outweigh the benefits of corn."

Esther looked at her sister as if she'd just committed blasphemy. "It's not our place to say what's important or not important to the historical society, Ida," she proclaimed fiercely. "Some people might consider even the most miniscule detail of Grandfather James's life of utmost interest!"

Ida threw Emily a mischievous wink, then provided her with the perfect atmosphere to escape unnoticed. "Horsefeathers!" she exclaimed spiritedly as she slid into the breakfast nook on the opposite side of the table from her outraged sister. "Only a complete dolt would find that sort of nonsense interesting."

Zack was running way behind schedule, but since Marnie had joined his household and taken over Angela's morning routine, he'd forgotten how much his little girl liked to dawdle when the people around her were most in a hurry. She also loved playing with his shaving cream, which was why he had to use one hand to shave and the other to keep ten chubby fingers from scooping dollops of lather out of the sink. He hoped the camera crew who were videotaping the Cougars' first intrasquad scrimmage today wouldn't take any close-ups of the broadcast booth. The last thing he wanted to do during his first practice session as a local television commentator was explain why he had three adhesive strips stuck to his chin.

"Why did I ever agree to take on this stupid job?" he asked a few moments later, glad to find that the bleeding had finally stopped as he ripped the adhesives off his face and tucked his squirming daughter under his right arm so that she couldn't attempt a backward somersault on their trip downstairs. "Because way down deep I'm a coward," he answered himself. "And I don't have the guts to tell anyone that what I really want to do is hide myself away from the public eye and write mysteries. The press boys would have a real good laugh over that one, wouldn't they?"

Right on cue, Angela giggled, and Zack scowled down at her as they reached the bottom step. "Thanks for your loving support, poppet."

"I's a pip," Angela agreed and scampered away to see what other kinds of trouble she could get into before her father left the house.

Since it took him an additional five minutes to scrub all the crayon marks off the kitchen door, the collar on Zack's white shirt was still turned up and his tie was dangling around his neck when the front doorbell rang. "My Em!" Angela screeched in delight, darting between Zack's legs as she took off down the hallway.

The sound that heralded his savior's arrival elated Zack as much as it did his daughter, but when he pulled open the door to greet the woman, he couldn't find the right words to say to her or force himself to move out of the way so that she could step inside. The smiling female who was standing outside on his doorstep resembled his next-door neighbor, but he couldn't quite believe it was actually her.

Those long legs looked familiar, but the Emily Hartcourt he knew didn't possess that pouty upper lip or that long exquisitely slender neck, and unless he'd been blind the last time he'd seen her, she couldn't possibly own that wild mane of golden-brown curls, that miniscule waist or that generous bosom. Then the imposter said hello to him in a husky voice that Zack recognized as Emily's, and he was left with no choice but to believe that she really did possess a mind-boggling array of previously hidden assets.

"Have I come on the wrong day?" Emily inquired anxiously when it began to look as if Zack wasn't expecting her and didn't quite know how to tell her she'd made a mistake. "Didn't you say you were starting work at WCLN *this* Wednesday?"

Zack couldn't seem to stop himself from staring at her beautiful mouth, which was outlined so delectably in pink. "Uh-huh," he murmured vaguely, then he saw Angela poking her head between his knees and realized that he was behaving like an idiot. He stepped aside hastily. "And you've arrived right on time, thank the Lord."

As she bent down to pick up a beaming Angela, Emily noticed that Zack's shirt was misbuttoned and that he was wearing one black sock and one gray one, which definitely helped to explain his shell-shocked expression. "Maybe I should come a half hour earlier tomorrow to keep Angela occupied while you get dressed," she offered sympathetically, but her tone was slightly baiting as she pointed to his feet. "You seem to be suffering from a slight coordination problem this morning."

Zack's ability to make swift mental adjustments was the reason he'd been so successful as a quarterback, but his reaction to the discovery that Emily Hartcourt had much more to offer than a sharp mind and a clever tongue was definitely slow in coming. That realization had finally arrived, however, and since her last remark proved that she enjoyed thinking of him as somewhat less than competent, the need to impress her with some fancy intellectual footwork came right along with it. Unfortunately both time and circumstances were working against him this morning, but one day in the very near future, Zack promised himself, he was going to knock his knockout of a neighbor for a real loop.

"I'd appreciate it if you could show up a bit earlier tomorrow," he conceded grudgingly, then sighed. "I guess I'd better go change my socks."

On his way upstairs he noticed that his shirt was buttoned wrong and his mouth tightened with annoyance. "Great!" he muttered sarcastically, realizing he had a long way to go before he'd be able to prove a thing to the amused female downstairs. As far as she was able to tell, the great Zoomer Petty was barely capable of dressing himself.

Ten minutes later, Emily boosted Angela up to the large front windows so she could watch her daddy

burn rubber as he screeched out of the driveway.
"Somebody definitely woke up on the wrong side of
the bed this morning," she concluded tartly. "But
even so, he might have been nice enough to notice that
I'm no longer dressing like a frump."

Then, struggling off an irrational twinge of disap-
pointment, she carried Angela into the great room,
opened the toy box and was thereby introduced to a
veritable crowd of stuffed animals. "So, my Em, you
be the baby and I'll be the mommy," Angela declared, setting down the new set of ground rules under which she expected them to operate since they were
now on her territory. To Emily's dismay, it took them
almost twenty minutes to complete their negotiations
to Angela's satisfaction, and another hour for her to
realize that being declared the baby meant she'd come
out on the strong end of their agreement. In Angela's
book, the mommy always did what she was told.

By the end of the day, Emily was completely worn
out, but she didn't feel anywhere near as exhausted as
Zack appeared to be that evening when he came
through the front door. Eyes downcast, shoulders
slumped, he didn't even notice that Emily was seated
on the couch in the great room, holding his sleeping
daughter in her lap until she said hello to him.

"Mmm," Zack grunted ungraciously, wrenching
off his tie and unbuttoning his shirt collar as he left the
foyer.

Apparently, watching football all day from an air-
conditioned broadcast booth took a harsh toll on a
man, Emily observed, and it had also done wretched
things to his blue linen jacket and pleated trousers.

Rumpled would be a kind description of his suit, but it was also an apt word to describe his hair. To Emily's dismay, she discovered that there was something vastly appealing about a man who had a large mustard stain on his white shirt, slightly bloodshot blue-green eyes and blond rumpled hair, especially when that man was considered by many to be a perfect specimen of contemporary manhood.

Unfortunately Zack misinterpreted her bemused expression and scowled across the room at her. "Don't say it!" he warned ominously, throwing up one hand to ward off her curious questions and using the other to fling his car keys onto the coffee table. "I've already endured enough abuse for one day and I'm in no mood to take any more!"

Emily arched her brows, but remained obediently silent. Angela, however, woke up at the gruff sound of his voice, bolted off Emily's lap and shot forward to tackle him around the knees. "Chickanuggets now, Daddy?" she squealed delightedly, reminding him of the promise he'd made to take her out to supper before leaving that morning. "And fries and shakes and toys and my faborites!"

The look Zack sent over Angela's head was so beseeching that Emily found herself rushing to the rescue without his having to ask, which if she'd stopped to think about it was exactly how she'd gotten herself hired as his baby-sitter in the first place. "Would you like me to take Angela to the drive-through at the Chicken Barn and pick up an order for you while you shower and change clothes? That should put her off for another fifteen minutes or so."

"After the day I've had, I'd be thankful for any break I could get, but are you sure you wouldn't mind?" Zack inquired, the overwhelming gratitude in his eyes making her feel like a modern version of Florence Nightingale.

"I'd be happy to," Emily replied, hoping her smile didn't look too sappy as she reached for Angela's hand and stood up. "C'mon, kiddo. Let's you and I go for a drive."

Zack was amazed by how easily Angela accepted the change in plans, but he was too grateful to question his daughter's newfound flexibility. If the normally rigid toddler was willing to follow Emily's lead, he was more than willing to let her, and with any luck, by the time the two of them returned, he'd be feeling halfway human again, have a better handle on how to deal with the huge mistake he'd made in agreeing to give sports broadcasting a try.

"You can take my car. The seat for Angela is in the trunk," he told Emily, bending down wearily to pick up his keys, but when he tried to hand them to her, she shook her head.

"No way! Unlike Angela, I have no desire to race cars in the Indy 500," she informed him emphatically. "I'll take my boring dependable sedan, thank you."

Zack opened his mouth to remind her that she still needed to take the car seat, and was thoroughly taken aback when Emily squared her slender shoulders and lifted her chin. "I know that must make me seem like a real old fuddy-duddy to you," she burst out defensively. "But I don't care what you think. I wouldn't

feel safe driving that roaring black monster anywhere, especially not with a baby in the car!''

"Hey!" Zack exclaimed, bringing both hands up in
a self-protective gesture. "I wasn't thinking any such
thing. If you want to take your own car, that's fine
with me. I was just going to remind you to pick up the
car seat."

"Oh," Emily replied in a deflated tone, but then she
noticed that the creases around his dimples had deep-
ened and she wanted to smack him. "Very well, then,"
she declared huffily, as if he was the one who'd just
made an utter fool of himself. "If that's all you intended to say, I'll go get my car."

"Why don't you order a family-size bucket with all
the fixings," Zack surprised himself by suggesting, but
all of a sudden he was very curious to find out whether
or not she had the guts to sit down at the same table
with him. "The least I can do to repay this favor is
spring for your supper, too—that is, if you wouldn't
mind sharing a meal with us."

An emphatic *no!* was on the tip of Emily's tongue,
but then she saw the challenging glint in his aquamarine eyes and she bit back her instinctive reply. So Mr.
God's Gift to Women didn't think a nerd like her
possessed the pluck to take him up on that challenge,
did he? Well, he was about to learn that he didn't
know half as much about her as he obviously thought
he did. "That sounds great," she replied with com-
mendable smoothness. "We should be back in about
twenty minutes."

"I'll be waiting," he retorted silkily, fascinated by the hot color that instantly rose in her cheeks, a telling blush that made him grin even wider.

"Fine," Emily exclaimed indignantly, quickly turning her back on him, but she was acutely aware of his eyes following her as she walked out of the room, and that awareness made her body ache in places it had rarely ached before, and never with such humiliating intensity. Fists clenched, she cursed herself for feeling sensations she didn't want to feel, then damned the hateful man staring after her for being able to excite her so easily.

When Zack heard the front door slam, a rush of energy pumped through his body, revitalizing him. According to all indications, Emily Hartcourt was fast becoming aware that physical chemistry was a force outside her control. Oh, yes, she was still fiercely determined to dislike him, but she was also strongly attracted to him, and that knowledge made the prospect of disarming her all the more enjoyable.

As he sprinted up the stairs to take his shower, Zack felt better than he had all day. Maybe he'd never be at ease behind a microphone, but he could think of several things to say to a skittish woman that would make her relax in his company and several more that would make relaxation impossible. In fact, he couldn't wait for Emily to get back with their supper so that he could divert himself from the daunting truth he had to face concerning his life after football for just a short while longer.

He was still entertaining himself with a picture of how she'd react the first time he kissed her when he realized how long it had been since any woman had inspired him to instigate such a calculated pursuit. Actually, upon further consideration, he had to admit that he'd never been required to do the chasing. The girls had started calling him way back in junior high school and they'd kept right on calling him until he'd joined the varsity.

At that point, everyone had expected the head cheerleader and the star quarterback to be a couple, so he and Shirley had done the expected thing and gone steady for the next three years. Even after he'd gotten married, however, he'd had to constantly fend off willing women who couldn't understand why his wedding vows should stop him from sleeping with them, and ever since word had gotten around about his separation and divorce, he'd become a hunted man.

"That's why I'm getting such a charge out of provoking Emily," he mused out loud, not sure he liked the thought that he might be suffering from a case of arrested adolescent development, but forced to concede the possibility. "For the first time in my life, I'm dealing with a woman who doesn't want to be caught, and that's what makes her such a challenge."

A challenge he had no intention of letting pass, Zack realized, even if he was being self-indulgent and his motivations were based on some primitive need to be the hunter for once, instead of the game. To justify his ruthless actions, all he had to remember was that his unsuspecting female quarry had been deprived of some highly essential lessons herself during her formative years, and even if his relationship with her never developed into anything permanent, he'd still be doing her a major favor by teaching her a few things about the wonderful world of passion. Holding firm to that admittedly chauvinistic conviction, Zack pulled on the faded pair of old jeans that had successfully drawn Emily's reluctant eyes below his waist on the day they'd first met, and a tight navy T-shirt that was practically guaranteed to attract a sexually repressed female's gaze to a well-developed set of biceps and pectorals.

Half an hour later, Zack leaned his shoulders against the back of his chair and bit into a spicy chicken leg, gratified by the positive results he'd obtained with such meager bait. Emily's flustered gaze had followed his every movement since she'd entered his kitchen, and she'd practically choked on her French fries when his forearm had "accidentally" brushed against the side of her breast as he'd reached across her to refill Angel's plastic Snoopy cup.

After that, each time he allowed his glance to stray lower than her neck, which it did with increasing regularity, her cheeks bloomed with hot color. A kinder man might have been satisfied with that, but after the rotten day he'd had, Zack didn't feel like being kind. He felt like reaching out and taking what he wanted, and he wanted to get even more of a rise out of Crabapple Lane's resident ice maiden.

Seeing that she'd yet to serve herself any chicken, he let his eyes stray once more to the modest vee of her blouse and inquired with a wolfish grin, "Breast or thigh?" deciding that an atmosphere that was already highly charged could withstand still another jolt.

No one was more surprised than he was when a pair of dark eyes collided with his over the top of the chicken bucket and Zack realized that the color in Emily's cheeks wasn't caused by the heat of excitement at all, but by anger. "I realize that some athletes require constant stimulation in order to function at top form, Mr. Petty," she stated caustically. "But I'm sure your regular bimbos would appreciate those sophomoric tactics of yours far more than I do."

"My regular bimbos! Now wait just a damned min—"

"I doubt you'll have to wait even that long if you return any of the heartfelt messages left on your answering machine. Buffy and Sally in particular sounded breathlessly eager to keep that colossal ego of yours overinflated."

Zack winced at that damning bit of information and could feel his ears turning red. "For your information, Emily, I don't know any Buffy or Sally, which is why I always keep my answering machine turned on. To keep strange women from getting through to me."

Emily rolled her eyes at that ridiculous claim. "Come now," she chided. "By your standards, I'm sure I seem naive, but I'm not stupid."

"You're naive by anyone's standards," Zack retorted, outraged by her contemptuous expression. "And any woman with an ounce of brains would recognize an obscene phone call when she heard one!"

"After the lecherous way you've been acting tonight, you honestly expect me to believe that you're just an innocent victim?" Emily demanded, unaware that her voice had risen to such a high pitch until she noted a movement out of the corner of her eye. Angela had hopped down from the table, her hands clamped over her ears, her big blue eyes brimming with tears.

"All done!" the child exclaimed, not sure who was more to blame for upsetting her, but including both adults in her accusing gaze as she stamped her foot and burst out, "I not play you ever, ever again!"

Five

Since he'd made such a mess of things tonight, Zack knew he deserved far worse than the limited KP duty left for him to perform, but upon walking back into the kitchen, he saw that the table had already been cleaned up and all the leftover food put away. Emily was standing in front of the sink, washing Angela's cup and the silverware they'd used in place of the plastic utensils provided by the fast-food restaurant. "You're still here?" he asked gruffly.

Emily took her time acknowledging his presence behind her, but Zack saw none of the anger he was expecting when she turned around to face him. If anything, she looked even more guilty than he felt. "Is Angela all right?" she questioned anxiously. "Were you able to calm her down?"

Zack's jaw tensed as he geared himself up to apologize to her for behaving like such a jerk, but first he tried to alleviate her concern for his daughter. "She's watching a cartoon tape on the VCR, but her eyes were starting to droop when I left the room, so it won't be long before she's asleep."

"That's good. She didn't nap very long this afternoon, and I didn't insist the way a more experienced baby-sitter would have."

Sensing that the next thing she was going to tell him was that she was quitting, Zack didn't dare put his apology off any longer. He couldn't let her quit the job. Angela needed her, and he was also beginning to realize that he just might need her, too. He'd forgotten that her kind of woman actually existed in the world, but Emily Hartcourt was a genuinely nice person, and compassionate to the marrow of her bones.

"Emily," he said quickly before she could utter those fateful words that would cut her out of his life, "I owe you an apology. I don't know what got into me tonight, but it wasn't my intention to offend you. I'm really sorry."

Emily nodded as she hung the damp dish towel over the small wooden rack on the counter. "I'm the one who should be sorry for yelling at you that way in front of Angela," she insisted, pointing to the fresh pot of decaffeinated coffee she'd made in the automatic brewer. "I never meant to upset her. I . . . I realize how much she loves you and I should've known better than to attack you when she was sitting right there listening to every word."

"She's not listening now," Zack informed her soberly as he walked over to the counter and grabbed a mug. "So feel free to continue denigrating my character. I probably deserve everything you've got left to say."

Emily couldn't prevent herself from smiling at the small qualification he'd added to that self-condemning statement. "Probably?"

Startled by the gentle amusement in her voice, Zack glanced over his shoulder at her. "Okay," he acknowledged with a rueful grin. "Maybe it's more than probable."

The man was totally incorrigible, Emily realized, but for some reason, damn his gorgeous hide, that realization didn't make him seem any less attractive to her. "Maybe?"

Zack sighed, as if something he didn't much care to learn about himself had just dawned on him. Then he reclaimed the chair he'd occupied at supper and asked Emily to pour herself a cup of coffee and join him. As soon as she was seated across from him at the table, he acknowledged sheepishly, "Guess I've started believing all the hype that's been written about me, haven't I?"

"You do seem to have a bit of difficulty admitting that you just might, probably, be wrong about something," Emily agreed, although she smiled at him when she said it. "Of course, it's easy to understand why you'd feel that way. According to Ida, you became a shining star in high school and have remained a star ever since."

Zack's expression turned thoughtful, then he seemed to arrive at some conclusion that pleased him immensely and his blue eyes twinkled across the table at her. "Which is why I need you even more than Angela does."

Emily didn't understand his logic. "Why would you think that?"

"Because I want to grow up to be a nice man, and to do that, I need someone around who's not afraid to pull my clay feet back to the ground and force my swelled head out of the clouds. At least," he amended dryly, "every once in a while."

Emily laughed, unaware that her eyes had left his face in order to scan a body that was definitely not that of a boy. Zachary Petty was a mature well-developed man. His shoulders were massive, the heavy muscles easily discernable beneath his navy T-shirt, and although her appreciative gaze couldn't travel below the level of the table, she already knew that his waist was narrow, his stomach flat and his thighs rock hard beneath those snug jeans. To be honest, Emily thought, she wasn't above feeling a little hero worship herself, but she was totally stunned when Zack's voice echoed her private thoughts.

"It wouldn't hurt you to be as honest with yourself as I'm trying to be about myself," he drawled wickedly. "Admit that you need something from me almost as desperately as I need your objectivity."

"And what would that be?" Angela inquired reluctantly, trying to sound sarcastic but very much afraid that the noticeable huskiness in her voice had ruined the effect.

Then to her dismay, Zack stood up from the table and came around to her side. He gazed down at her, his smile encouraging her to do something, but she wasn't sure what that something was and feared he was about to take the decision out of her hands. "All you have to do is stand up," he assured her, reaching down to encircle her slender wrist with his warm fingers. "And I'll do all the rest."

"All..." She tried to swallow the nervous lump in her throat, but it wouldn't budge. Zachary Petty intended to kiss her! Even without verbal confirmation she knew that, but she couldn't just let him pull her up out of her chair as if she wanted to be in his arms as much as he seemed willing to position her there. "All the rest of... of what?"

"This for starters," Zack informed her, his mesmerizing gaze beckoning her to surrender her will to him, which she couldn't seem to prevent herself from doing, as slowly but surely, he drew her up by her wrist to stand in front of him. "And then there's this," he murmured softly, splaying one hand behind her waist to bring her another step closer.

He was so much taller than she was that Emily had to tilt her face up to gaze into his eyes, which she did, entranced by the warm sparks of color that flickered in them, brilliant green flames that burned hotter and hotter the longer she stared into them, until there was no blue left to be seen. Then the hand at her back drew her lower body into searing contact with a pair of hard masculine thighs, and her gasp provoked a knowing smile that played at the corners of his mouth and drew her helpless gaze to his lips.

Zack gave her a tiny sample of what she could expect in moments to come, brushing her trembling lips with a soft kiss. But before he claimed her mouth in the way her eyes told him she really wanted, he indulged an insistent need of his own. He let his gaze fall to her graceful shoulders and down the bodice of her blouse to her long shapely legs, then back up slowly, past her slender neck and over the delicate planes of her face to her soft mouth, her high cheekbones, the uncontrollable curls that caressed her forehead, to the incredibly long lashes over her brandy-colored eyes.

"Zack! I don't think—"

"Shh," he said softly, touching her mouth with one long finger.

He was no longer smiling and when she saw the darkening intense gleam in his eyes, she sucked in her lower lip. Suddenly she felt more threatened than she ever had in her life. "You mustn't—"

"You're a beautiful woman, professor," he whispered, bending. "And it amazes me that you don't seem to realize that."

Emily knew she should move, push him away, but her hands flattened helplessly on the front of his T-shirt and she felt solid muscle and heat against her cold fingers. His breath teased her lips as he poised his mouth over hers.

"No," she protested weakly and tried to move away, but his hips pressed her against the edge of the table and the twisting motion of her body provoked a shocking reaction in him that she had never expected to provoke in any man, let alone one who could have any woman he wanted.

Zack drew in a sharp breath, and his hand tightened at the side of her waist. "Lord," he murmured in astonishment. "It's been one hell of a lot of years since a woman's excited me as much as you have."

Emily felt as if her entire body was blushing, but the real shocker arrived when his mouth covered hers. She felt a searing heat that radiated downward from her head to her feet, then pooled around her ankles until her toes tried to curl up inside her sandals. She felt dizzy, weak with terror, but at the same time, giddy with anticipation. Something wild was about to happen, an overwhelming explosion that was only seconds away from ignition, but then Zack's lips relented slightly, relieving some of the rapidly building pressure.

Emily didn't know how, but he seemed to sense her anxiety, her reluctance to unleash the tempest of need that was gathering such incredible force inside her, yet when he drew away to search her face for a moment, she didn't see anything in his features that indicated a desire to stop the coming storm. What she saw there was supreme masculine triumph.

"I knew it," he murmured hoarsely. "Beneath that straitlaced exterior lies a passionate hot-blooded temptress...." He gazed into her shell-shocked eyes, smiling at the impatience and hunger that was as easy to read there as her bafflement. "Don't worry, sweetheart, just relax and let go. I'm as eager to feel all that pent-up passion inside you as you are to let me."

Before she could deny it, he lowered his head again and traced her bottom lip with his teeth, slowly, gently, in a masterful exploration that was beyond anything she'd ever experienced with a man. Her fingers clenched his T-shirt, and the hot shivers started up inside her body again, making her tremble and burn. He knew ways of using his mouth that she'd never imagined in her wildest fantasies. He was also an expert at coaxing her to respond to his instructions. His tongue teased and his mouth demanded, and she answered each and every demand, completely at his mercy.

"Yes, like that," he encouraged into her breathlessly parted lips. "Kiss me back. A little more, honey. I want more..."

Emily couldn't even think about holding back. His tongue probed inside her mouth, tasting her with a rhythm that built and built as his shameless fingers trespassed under her arms, his thumbs caressing the curving undersides of both breasts, until her nipples were throbbing with an urgency that made her cry out. Even so, her body jerked in shock when she felt his warm hands on her bare skin, and her eyes flew open.

"I know," he murmured soothingly, and his mouth touched her eyelids, closing them. "I won't hurt you. Don't be scared."

Emily wasn't just scared, she was terrified, but then his large warm hands closed over her breasts, and wave after wave of pleasure exploded in every cell of her body. She threw her head back and her spine arched and when his hands contracted, she almost fainted.

"Lord," Zack breathed reverently, as deeply shaken by her ardent response as she was.

The generous curves that swelled above the delicate lace of her bra felt like silk beneath his fingers. She was so soft, her skin smooth and warm, yet the tips were tight and hard in his palms. He couldn't wait to see her breasts, taste them for the first time, but he didn't dare take that kind of risk with her now, not when her fear was running as close to the surface as her passion. So he kissed her soft mouth instead, then kissed her again and again until he was so far gone that his daughter's voice barely got through to him.

"Her a nice Em to hug, Daddy," Angela proclaimed happily, then made sure her presence was acknowledged by squeezing herself between them and clasping one arm around each of their legs. "Me a hug, too," she demanded, completely oblivious to the acute tension in the atmosphere.

Emily was not only startled by the child's arrival, she was mortified. Her face burned and her lips trembled and she didn't know where to look. Zack made a rough sound under his breath, but he didn't appear to be any too steady, either, or prepared to shift gears so abruptly.

Zack cleared his throat, then was forced to clear it again before he could get any words out. "I thought you were sleeping, poppet."

"I's awake!" Angela declared, releasing her grip on Emily so she could wrap her small body even more tightly around her father's knee.

"She's awake," Zack repeated stupidly and Emily smiled overbrightly as if he'd just made a brilliant deduction.

"I, uh... I guess I'd better get going," she stammered, in a tone as taut and desperate as the expression in her downcast eyes. She took a step backward, away from him, then another and another, until she was finally near enough to the back door to make a run for it. "I told my aunts I'd be home around six, and they're probably starting to worry."

Perceptive little creature that she was, Angela waved her hand at Emily's swiftly retreating form. "Bye-bye, my Em."

Although her hand was already turning the doorknob, Emily paused. "Bye, sweetie. I'll see you in the morning." But then, before Zack could express his relief that she wasn't planning to quit on him or even say a single word, she was out the door and gone.

"Bye-bye, my Em," he murmured hoarsely, as he reached down to pick up Angela.

"Her mine, not yours," his daughter informed him tartly, but she cushioned the blow by pressing a sloppy kiss on the side of his neck.

"Not quite yet," Zack agreed, casting one more longing look at the door, before shutting off the lights and striding out of the room. "But now that I know one or two of her weak spots, it's only a matter of time."

Angela pointed to the pink polka dots on her pajamas. "I's got spots."

"Very pretty," Zack complimented, but even though he loved his daughter with all his heart, thoughts about another female kept him distracted for the rest of the night. Since Angela was used to being the sole center of his attention, she refused to go to sleep until well past eleven.

It took Zack even longer than that to finally settle down, but when he answered the door the next morning, he could see that Emily had missed out on her normal amount of rest, as well, which put him in a much better mood than the one he'd been in ever since his alarm had gone off. In his opinion those faint purple smudges beneath her brown eyes and the slightly bruised look of her mouth added an extra touch of beauty to her face. Perhaps he felt that way about it because he was the man responsible for both those things, and that knowledge gave him a great deal of pleasure.

"Rough night?" he inquired, striving for an innocent expression, but failing miserably.

Somewhere around three in the morning, Emily had decided that the best way to handle facing this man again was to pretend that nothing really earth-shattering had happened between them last night. They were both normal healthy adults and, like countless of other men and women around the world who didn't know each other very well, they'd satisfied a natural curiosity by sharing a few meaningless kisses. To her dismay, however, all it took was one glance from those devilish blue-green eyes of his to utterly destroy that rationale, and her composure disintegrated at the same time.

"Must you look so insufferably pleased with yourself!" she exclaimed indignantly. "It's not as if you scored a touchdown or something!"

Zack supposed that the football metaphor was an effort on her part to remind him of how little respect she had for the petty triumphs enjoyed by professional athletes, but he found her scathing rebuke vastly amusing. "I can tell that you haven't watched me play very often. Otherwise you'd know that achieving a

first down made me almost as happy as getting into the
end zone.''

Emily didn't think she'd live to see the day when
some hulking brute of a man would compare making
love to her with gaining yardage on a football field,
and the insulting correlation outraged her so much
that she couldn't speak. Zack, unfortunately, seemed
happy to fill in the silence with another round of his
outrageous teasing.

''You know why? Because with every first down,
I'm rewarded with four more chances to reach the goal
line.''

Emily had heard quite enough, but she was no
match for him when it came to football analogies or
sexual innuendos, and his dancing eyes proclaimed
that humiliating truth with a satisfaction that made
her teeth grit. ''Where's Angela?'' she asked tightly,
stepping deliberately around him.

Zack grinned. ''As yet, there's been no noise from
our pint-size cheering section.''

Emily whirled back to face him, thoroughly incensed, but Zack didn't wait around to see the results
of his parting shot. Some men were smart enough to
know when they were pressing their luck, and he was
really pushing the odds by reminding her of Angela's
imprudent arrival in the kitchen last night.

''If you don't mind listening for her to wake up,'' he
called back over his shoulder as he sauntered toward
the kitchen. ''I'm going to finish my cup of coffee,
then head out to the studio.''

''Mountain-grown hemlock, I pray,'' she called
back sweetly, but the only reply she got to that was a

low sexy chuckle that inspired such a hot shiver of awareness inside her that her knees turned to water and she had to grope her way over to the closest chair.

"Damn him!" she groused, her inability to control her embarrassing physical reactions to him making her feel infinitely sorry for herself.

"I like you, too," Zack said on his way back through the room. Then, just in case she didn't believe him, he dropped down on one knee and pressed a brief kiss on her startled mouth before continuing on his way. At the front door, he paused only long enough to flash his dimples at her and say, "See you later."

"Not if I see you first," Emily retorted, but it was a trite comeback and didn't show half the imagination he had with his suggestive remarks about the first downs and end zones, a realization that was extremely unnerving. She was beginning to suspect that most of the preconceived notions she'd had about professional athletes, Zoomer Petty in particular, were about as reliable as Aunt Ida's homemade spring elixir, and if she continued to swallow them, she was going to end up in bed suffering from something far more devastating than a queasy stomach.

Even more daunting was the knowledge that the bed she ended up in would not be her own.

Zack yanked off his headset, waited for the director to signal a mock commercial, then swung his upholstered chair around to face Frank Cooper, the hatchet-faced but dulcet-toned man who'd been the "voice" of the Cougars for the past eight years.

"Have I managed to convince *you*, yet, Frank?" he demanded. "Or are you still holding firm to the company line?"

Unable to hide his mottled complexion or ignore the rivulets of sweat that dripped down his receding brow onto his deeply creased forehead, Frank sighed in surrender. "Okay. Okay! You're lousy at this. Is that what you want me to say? Listening to you is about as much fun as reading aloud from the phone book, and filling in all the blanks in your commentary is making me nuts."

Zack gazed up at the tinted glass panel behind him. "Did you hear that, Ed? I'm driving Frank nuts."

A disembodied voice floated down from on high. "I heard him, but I still can't believe this is really happening. You've got the knowledge we need, a great voice, and the book on you says you're a real fast study."

"Which just goes to show that a man can't always believe what he reads," Zack retorted, sensing he was finally getting somewhere with Edward Baxter, the bullheaded station owner.

"With you on board, our female viewership will increase by the thousands!"

"They're only going to see me once or twice during the game," Zack argued. "And watching me sweat bullets because I'm terrified of a microphone is bound to be a real turnoff."

Frank put in helpfully. "He's got you there, Ed."

"All you've got to do is say the word," Zack promised, "and I'll rip up our contract."

"Hell! I can't do that!"

Frank leaned over the broadcast table and suggested under his breath, "Repeat that story about Coach Williams placing Boom Boom Taylor on the injured reserve list. Trust me. That long drawn out saga will push him right over the edge."

Zack scowled, striving for an affronted expression. "I thought that was one of my best stories."

"It was," Frank stated dryly.

Ed's booming voice interrupted their laughter. "I don't see why you guys find this situation so damned funny! The preseason starts next week and my advertisers are expecting Zoomer Petty to co-anchor the game. If you're not in that broadcast booth, Zack, they're going to raise so much cain I'll be lucky to get fifty cents for a minute of airtime."

"Not if you send them a tape of this rehearsal," Zack predicted. "Let them hear me doing voice-overs during their commercials."

"Hell!"

Frank's smooth baritone bounced off the walls, making every microphone screech in protest. "How many times did he make this happen today, Ed? If we'd really been on the air, those he didn't bore to death with his monotone would be switching off their sets to keep from going deaf."

"We've already got him on the run, pal," Zack admonished, clearing his much maligned throat. "Let's not get carried away."

"Just trying to help out, son," Frank assured him, and then Ed's hollow voice came down around their heads, sounding a death knell. "Sorry, Zack, but you're outa here."

"Yes!" Zack leapt out of his chair, thrust both arms in the air victoriously, then reached down to shake Frank's hand. "I owe you one, buddy. Any time you want me for an interview, I'll be here with bells on!"

Frank appeared to seriously consider that offer, then nodded his bald head. "Sounds fair to me. Whenever you open your mouth, we'll just turn down the sound and rely on closed captions."

Six

Zack drove away from the station feeling as if he didn't have a care in the world. Then it dawned on him that if he didn't have a job to go to, Emily would quickly point out that he didn't need a baby-sitter, and that presented a problem that occupied his mind all the way to route 23. If he was actually going to pursue his childhood dream and try his hand at writing, he couldn't have any distractions, and Angela didn't know how to be anything else. Beyond that, he liked the idea of having a sweet caring woman like Emily in his house, enjoyed picturing her there with his daughter, showing her interest in everything Angela did, teaching her the difference between the way males and females operated.

No, he decided, he couldn't take the risk of telling Emily that he'd quit his job and would be working at home from now on, which meant that he'd have to stick to the routine he'd already established with her. As for his premature arrival today, he'd tell her that he'd finished his pregame preparations for tomorrow's scrimmage and had, therefore, been able to leave the studio early. He knew that Emily would likely react to that information by leaving him and Angela to their own devices for the remainder of the afternoon, which was just fine with him. As soon as Angela went down for her nap, he'd haul his word processor out to the gardener's cottage and set up a place for himself to write. Once that was done, all he'd have to worry about was sneaking out there every morning without being seen and arriving back in the house each night looking as if he'd just put in a normal day at the office. Since Emily's interest in football would fit on the head of a pin, she'd never find out that he was missing from the broadcast booth.

To Zack's relief, everything went according to plan, at least up to the point where he was able to clean out a cozy space for himself in the cottage. He'd just carried in his computer table and was checking out the electrical outlets when he saw a flash of blue at the rear window and realized that someone was spying on him. He also knew that someone's fascination with football could disrupt all his plans!

"Ida!" he called out, before the snoopy old woman could duck back behind the hedge. "Could you come in here a second?"

To her credit, the elderly female didn't look the slightest bit abashed as she rounded the corner of the cottage and stepped inside the door. "Good afternoon, Zoomer,'' she greeted him smilingly. "Is this how you intend to spend all the spare time you've got on your hands now? Fixing up the old homestead?''

Zack's eyes narrowed on her wrinkled face. He was annoyed by the self-satisfied smile that toyed at the corner of her cupid's-bow mouth, but doubly annoyed with himself for not realizing that his departure from WCLN would immediately be announced over the airwaves. For a few seconds, he thought about denying the news item, which was, he now realized, what Ida had come over to verify. But then he looked into a pair of snapping brown eyes, eyes that reminded him very much of Emily's, and decided that to insult this woman's obvious, if previously unsuspected, intelligence, would only be a waste of time.

Instead he inquired bluntly, "Does Emily know I've quit?''

"Of course not,'' Ida replied. "She's far too distracted by the knowledge that she's physically attracted to a know-nothing jock to pay any attention to the news, though she might come out of her tizzy long enough to wonder what's going on when all those reporters start showing up here.''

The woman's contention that Emily's attraction to him threw her into a tizzy made Zack grin, but then he digested the rest of her statement. "Damn! I didn't even think about that!''

"I take it, then, that I was right to assume that you would prefer it if Emily didn't find out that you're unemployed and that this computer setup has something to do with that?''

"You assume right," Zack conceded, astonished by her perception, and then, to his further amazement, he found himself confiding his innermost hopes and dreams to a little old lady with blue hair, who as far as he knew spent half her time puttering around in an herb garden and the other half peering at his house through the hedge.

"So you want to be a writer," Ida commented thoughtfully once he'd finished baring his soul. She tapped two fingers on the side of her cheek and declared, "Well, this really should be quite easy to pull off, Zachary. I have several errands that will keep Emily busy for the remainder of the day, and filching tomorrow morning's paper before she sees it will be a piece of cake. Emily never watches any television before the eleven o'clock news and she always goes up to bed before the sports comes on. If you answer all the reporters' questions today, I'm sure their interest in this story will swiftly die down, and as soon as that happens, most of our worries will be over."

"Our worries?" Zack inquired, his expression conveying both his relief and his dumbfounded reaction to acquiring such an unlikely ally.

"I want to see my niece happy," Ida declared forthrightly. "She has a great many things to offer a man, but you're the first one who's showed any interest in finding out what makes her tick. The only thing those pseudo-intellectuals she associates with at the college are able to see in her is her worthiness for tenure. I'm none too sure any of those wimps are aware that she's a beautiful woman, and the couple of them who have looked beyond her brains aren't the kind of man she needs."

Ida's tone was fierce, and Zack swallowed hard, hating to admit that he might not be any better for Emily than those pseudo-intellectuals. "I'm not making any promises here, Ida. At this point in our relationship, marriage isn't a part of the picture. What I feel for Emily is, well, it's..."

Ida smiled at the dishonorable truth he couldn't quite bring himself to say to a woman of her advanced years. "Purely physical, I know, but I also know that wherever the body leads, the heart generally follows."

"Sometimes, maybe," Zack admitted, beginning to suspect that he could be totally honest with this woman and not offend her, yet hardly able to believe such a thing was possible. Ida was old enough to be his grandmother, and he certainly couldn't picture himself discussing his sex life with that judgmental woman.

Ida finished the rest of his unspoken thought. "Other times, an affair is the only thing that develops out of a relationship."

"That's right," he agreed in a cautious tone.

"Emily could certainly use a hot passionate affair," Ida replied calmly, then laughed when she saw Zack's shocked expression. "I may be a spinster, Zack Petty, but I've had a few romantic flings in my day, and I don't regret a single one of them."

"I'm not so sure Emily shares your sophisticated view of life," Zack said.

But even though Ida agreed with him, she didn't see the harm in broadening her niece's horizon a little. "You should have seen that child before Esther started stifling all her natural spontaneity," Ida said. "It's no wonder Emily relates so well to Angela. When she first came to us, Emily was just like her."

Zack tried to picture straitlaced Emily racing through the halls of Hartcourt House, and even though he couldn't quite fit that image to the adult woman, he was willing to be convinced. "Tell me more about what she was like as a little girl," he requested, and in the brief time left to them before the local media started arriving, Ida happily complied.

After two weeks on the job, Emily realized that Angela required much more from a caretaker than balanced meals and a safe environment in which to play. Since it was equally obvious to her that the child's father didn't recognize that a gifted child had very special needs, she decided to take it upon herself to educate him. Maybe Angela's future welfare wasn't really any of her business, but that didn't stop Emily from caring for the little girl. Nor would it stop her from confronting Zack with the error of his ways.

A trip to the library had confirmed her conclusion about the unique problems posed by a gifted child, but it had also disclosed a few astonishing facts that required her to rethink her estimation of Zack. According to one of the books she'd read on the subject, giftedness did not necessarily restrict itself just to the mind. In addition to being born with more than their fair share of intelligence, the gifted were also often blessed with a natural athletic ability.

The author had gone on to say that since society admires the athlete far more than the intellectual, a smart little boy was likely to choose the route leading to the NFL or the NBA instead of the one leading to Mensa. Of course, upon reading this, Emily had to wonder if the man called Zoomer was in actuality a fully developed Zoon, a compound rather than a simple animal. Had his parents unconsciously suppressed the intellectual supremacy of their son because society found so much more to appreciate in his athletic prowess? Now that she'd gotten to know him better, Emily realized that possibility was highly probable.

Beyond that, if she was willing to examine a few of the other hints she'd been given recently but done her best to ignore, Emily had no choice but to accept the likelihood that there was much more between Zack's ears than two of the most gorgeous eyes she'd ever seen. Lately, in fact, she'd begun to suspect that those times he looked at her as if he didn't have the brains to follow her logic were, in reality, his way of punishing her for behaving like an intellectual snob.

Even more deflating was the realization that in some ways he was right to think of her as a snob. Though she'd only recently started questioning some of her personal viewpoints and philosophies, she'd already concluded that some of them had no rational basis and definitely needed changing. And who was responsible for provoking those kinds of questions in the first place? Emily asked herself. None other than Zack

Petty, that was who, the same man who had succeeded in tossing all of her comfortable daily sched-
ules into an uproar, manipulated her into putting all
her summer projects on hold in order to be his full-
time baby-sitter and, for all practical purposes, thoroughly disrupted her well-ordered life.

That being the case, how could she possibly hold on
to the ridiculous notion that he was all brawn and no
brains? No matter how badly she might prefer it to be
that way, Emily knew she couldn't afford to think
along those lines anymore. She was dealing with a
shrewd devious operator, and that realization forced
her to ask one more question: what was the real reason behind his interest in her?

And he was interested, she acknowledged with a
thrill of pleasure. Interested enough to flirt with her
and kiss her and stare brazenly at her, as if he
wanted—

Emily abruptly stopped this train of thought, reminding herself that what Zack Petty wanted from her
he'd probably already gotten from any number of the
empty-headed bimbos who dropped by the house occasionally unannounced or left him gushy messages on
his answering machine. Did she want to be like them,
just another notch on his bedpost?

Although she thought about that for several minutes, Emily couldn't quite convince herself that she
wouldn't adore having Zack Petty make love to her,
and the frustration she felt over this newly discovered
weakness in her character must have been readily apparent on her face, for Zack pounced on her the instant she walked through his front door.

"Loaded for bear already this morning are we, professor?" he observed irritably as he tucked his shirttails into his trousers. "What are you suggesting this time? In-depth psychological and intellectual testing? Montessori school? A live-in tutor who can push Angela to learn everything she needs to know in the shortest amount of time possible?"

Emily was not only thankful to find out that Zack hadn't evolved to the point where he could read minds, but she was happy to talk on a subject that had become very dear to her heart since she'd started working for him. Considering how often she'd confronted him with her unwelcome opinions during the past few days, she realized that she'd given him ample cause to assume that she'd never quit trying to persuade him to be more open-minded, to at least take a look at some of the fabulous educational opportunities available for gifted children, but for the first time since they'd started discussing Angela's seemingly endless capacity for learning, she also realized that Zack probably knew more about the subject than she could ever hope to learn.

"Are those some of the methods your parents chose to try out on you?" she asked, searching his face intently. "Is that why you're so dead set against treating Angela as anything else but a normal child?"

"She is a normal child!" Zack retorted harshly, but then the knowing expression on Emily's face got through to him and he didn't see much point in denying the truth any longer. "And yes, the reason I don't want anyone pinning labels on my daughter is because I know what being a freak of nature feels like.

If nothing else, I'm going to make sure that Angela isn't robbed of her childhood.''

"Like you were," Emily concluded gently.

Zack sighed. "Like I was."

"So you're a firm believer in the philosophy that the only thing a gifted child requires at this age is an environment that nurtures her curiosity and allows her to experiment with the world around her in an unstructured way?''

Zack's brows rose in surprise. "Do some of those books you've been reading actually contain a philosophy like that?''

Emily nodded. "There are some professionals out there who can see more than an IQ chart when they view a bright child," she admonished with a smile. "If you like, I could lend you a couple of their books so you could bring yourself up-to-date on the latest research.''

"In other words," Zack said in a teasing tone, "you've finally come to the conclusion that I might be smarter than you first thought, but when it comes to doing what's best for Angela, you still think I could stand to learn a thing or two.''

Emily shrugged, but didn't deny his conclusion. "It's my opinion that Angela could benefit greatly from having a father who keeps an open mind.''

"Okay, Em. You win. For Angel's sake, I'll read your books," Zack replied, though he made it plain that he was only conceding a minor skirmish in their battle, not an all-out surrender. "But if I don't like what I read, that will be the end of our discussion. Agreed?''

"Well . . ."

Zack scowled over at her as he picked up his suit coat from the table in the entryway. "Did anyone ever tell you that you can be a royal pain in the neck at times?"

Since she hadn't caused the slightest ripple to anyone's peace of mind for as long as she could remember, Emily's face lit up as if she'd just received a wonderful compliment. "Not lately," she admitted blithely. "But I appreciate your noticing my staunch efforts to change."

Zack stared at the mischievous sparkle in her dark eyes and found himself laughing. "Oh, I've noticed, all right," he declared hoarsely, then decided to make her aware that he was equally cognizant of some other changes. Like the fact that being out in the sunshine with Angela every day had added a warm peach glow to her flawless skin and that her wayward brown curls now contained several eye-catching streaks of glistening gold.

Emily noticed the sudden hot gleam in his eyes and could feel herself blushing before he stepped forward and confirmed that his thoughts were no longer focused on her personality. His appreciative gaze slipped lower, lingering for a few moments on the enticing neckline of her pink tank top, then sliding down to admire her matching shorts. "And since you've stopped hiding your figure beneath all those old-fashioned clothes, I've also noticed that you've got beautiful legs, spectacular breasts and a tight little—"

"Don't!"

Zack grinned, allowing her protest to stop him from saying such outrageous things, but reaching out at the same time and hauling her body against his. He looked at her until she lifted her head, and then he trapped her brown eyes with his. "Don't what?" He breathed against her mouth. "Don't do this?"

Emily gasped, but at the first touch of his lips, pleasure erupted within her in a blinding shower of bliss-filled sensations. Before she knew what she was doing, she reached up over his broad shoulders and curled her fingers around the strong column of his neck, pulling his face closer so that she could intensify the pressure of his mouth on hers.

Oh, yes, she'd wanted this, had yearned for it to happen again practically every moment since he'd kissed her the first time. To feel his warm lips moving over hers, his arms closing around her, was exactly what she wanted, and she never wanted these feelings to end. When her hips made contact with his hard thighs, Zack made a sound deep in his throat, and she gloried in that sound as much as she reveled in the urgent proof of his desire she could feel against her body. As unbelievable as it seemed to her, he wanted this, too!

When his tongue probed her mouth, a wild fire seared through her veins with a glorious heat. In his arms, Emily stopped being a thinking person. All she could do was surrender to her feelings, allowing all reason to flee and the unbearable pleasure to rush in. A sweet pulsing intensity throbbed through her as Zack pushed up her tank top and cupped her breasts in his palms.

"Lord, but you're firm," he murmured hoarsely. "If you were a bit more daring, you could go without a bra." He stroked a hardened nipple with his thumb. "If you had, I'd already have this tight bud inside my mouth."

His provocative words made the sensitive tips of her breasts contract even more, and Emily arched her back, telling him without words that the waiting was agony, that she didn't want any barriers between them. Then he released the center catch of her bra and his tongue replaced his fingers, giving her the added pleasure she was demanding. Her hands came up to clutch at his shoulders as a wild trembling began inside her, a delicious shaking that made her knees go weak.

Zack felt her trembling and knew that he'd have to stop soon, but his body was suffering from the same kind of exquisite torment as hers and he didn't want it to end. In the months since he'd regained custody of Angela, he'd dreamed about having a normal life, pictured himself and his daughter living in a nice big house on an ordinary street in an ordinary neighborhood. He'd also imagined some nameless faceless beauty who would take care of his daughter and bring him his pipe and slippers at night, but nothing in his imagination had prepared him for a woman who could make him feel like exploding just by emitting a soft sigh of pleasure. Emily Hartcourt could do that to him and more.

Like the woman he'd conjured up for himself in his imagination, she was sweet and incredibly responsive to his touch. He loved knowing he could incite such turbulent passion in her. He also knew she was astonished by the pleasure she felt, and her surprise delighted him, but even though he wanted her more than he could remember ever wanting another woman, including his wife, he didn't want to take advantage of her obvious inexperience. When Emily gave herself to him, he wanted her to be fully aware of what she was doing, to come to him for reasons that went far beyond physical desire.

Zack stiffened, and he broke off their embrace abruptly, staring blindly down into her startled eyes as he was hit by the truth of his own feelings. He wanted Emily Hartcourt to love him as honestly and completely as the woman he'd imagined in his dreams! To make love to him, not because he could arouse her so easily, but because she genuinely liked and accepted him as a person.

Yet, if he was ever going to attain that lofty expectation, Zack realized, he couldn't continue deceiving her. Thus far, she seemed to prefer the real Zachary Petty to the celebrity version, but before he got himself more deeply involved with her than he already was, he had to make certain that was so. It was up to him to show her who he really was beneath all the hype that had surrounded him almost since birth. Afterward, if she still liked what she saw, he would make her his, not just physically, but in every way there was.

Once that decision was made, Zack couldn't wait to put his thoughts into action, and he reached for Emily's wrist. "I need to show you something before Angela wakes up," he told her, hoping she'd understand why he'd been so reluctant to reveal himself to her before now, praying he'd finally found a woman he could really trust.

As for Emily, she felt as if the ground had suddenly been cut out from under her feet. One minute Zack was kissing her, driving her closer and closer to the point of no return, and the next he was pushing her away. Then, before she got the chance to voice her confusion, or even catch her breath, Zack was dragging her through the great room and into the kitchen.

A second later, she realized he was heading for the back door! Aware that Aunt Ida was already outside working in the herb garden, Emily tugged frantically at the hem of her tank top, making sure that she looked halfway decent even though her brain was swirling with dark murderous thoughts. For arousing her to the brink of total surrender, then changing gears on her in midstream, Zack Petty deserved to be shot.

"What do you think you're doing?" she hissed as he strode purposefully out the door without seeming to take any notice of her obvious reluctance to follow him. She tried to press home that point one more time by tugging harder on her captured wrist, but all Zack did was readjust his fingers into a tighter manacle and continue on his merry way.

"Will you please stop behaving like such a Neanderthal!" she exclaimed furiously, then to prevent herself from getting cracked in the head, she was forced to duck under the low-hanging branches of the spruce tree. Whereupon she noticed that they were headed toward the heavily wooded rear corner of his property, which she'd avoided on her daily walks with Angela because she knew there was a creek running through the ravine along the boundary line of his yard. The little girl might decide to explore it when Emily wasn't around to watch her.

Apparently Zack didn't harbor any similar concerns about the injuries she might suffer from being hauled through a thistle patch in her shorts. "Zachary! Where are you taking me?" she demanded, still not able to comprehend what on earth could possibly motivate him to forgo an extremely satisfying sensual interlude in favor of stalking willy-nilly through this prickly undergrowth.

"Patience, Em," Zack suggested. "I'm taking the shortcut, so you'll see soon enough."

"But the only thing back here to see is the ravine and old man Radford's empty carriage house."

Then they burst through a gap in the trees and Emily's mouth dropped open. "Oh, my," she whispered in delight as the tiny picturesque white cottage came into view. "I knew that there had been some work crews out here, but I didn't realize the extent of their project. You had this dilapidated old place completely remodeled, too?"

"Sure did. I thought a private hideaway might come in very useful one day for me and Angela," Zack informed her. "When she gets a little older she can use it for a playhouse, and when she gets to be a rebellious teenager, I can use it to get away from her."

"It looks like something straight out of *Hansel and Gretel,*" Emily said, as she stepped ahead of Zack onto the quaint red cobblestone path, which she could now see started at the side of his garage, then meandered in and out of the trees until it reached the cottage. She started dragging him along behind her. "Or *Snow White and the Seven Dwarfs.* I love that thatched-roof effect and those lead-paned windows, and the heart design on those shutters is absolutely darling. Actually the entire place is darling!"

"Darling is not quite the effect I was going for," Zack replied dryly, but he was so pleased by her enthusiastic reaction that he allowed her to take the lead without mentioning the fact that she seemed quite eager to use the same caveman tactics with him that she'd so hotly accused him of employing with her.

"I can't wait to see what you've done with the inside."

"I can't wait to show you."

A third voice was heard through a thick line of overgrown hedge. "Then I'd better go up to the house and keep an ear out for Angela. She'll be up soon and wanting her breakfast."

Knowing that her aunt was still up to her old bad habits and had probably been spying on them ever since they'd come out the back door, Emily wanted nothing more than to jump into the ravine and disappear from Zack's sight. To her amazement, however, he didn't seem to be the least bit annoyed at being the subject of the nosy woman's all-seeing eyes. "Thanks, pal," he called back to her. "Oh, and Ida, if Angel is up, would you mind fixing her some cereal and a piece of toast so that Emily and I can take our time out here?"

"Not at all, Zack," Ida shouted back, and although the woman had already put considerable distance between herself and them, Emily was almost certain that she heard a perfectly wicked sounding chuckle. "Take all the time you need, my boy, all the time you need."

Emily was totally flummoxed. As far as she knew, Zack had not had any contact with either one of her aunts since his return from London when they'd cornered him in the parlor and subjected him to an inquisition. "'Thanks, pal'?" she repeated his words incredulously. "You and Aunt Ida are friends?"

"We sure are," Zack confirmed, holding up his hand so that Emily could see that two of his fingers were tightly crossed. "Ida and I are just like this."

"Since when?"

"Since she agreed to share my deep dark secret," Zack replied, then made a sweeping gesture with his arm that welcomed her to step over the threshold and into the cottage. "And I'm hoping that sharing it with you will bring the two of us a lot closer, as well."

Seven

After Zack's intriguing comments, Emily didn't quite know what to expect when she walked into the cottage, but nothing she saw there looked like an answer to some deep dark mystery. As far as she could tell, Zack had been using the place for extra storage. Up between the exposed wooden rafters, she saw the end pieces for a swing set, a wide plank of plywood topped with short lengths of discarded lumber, a warped toboggan and several old-fashioned lanterns. When she surveyed the small main room, she saw a cluster of rattan porch furniture that had obviously seen better days, several piles of newspapers, two filing cabinets and a tall stack of cardboard packing boxes.

Then her gaze traveled to the rear wall beneath a large sparkling-clean window and she saw an open space eked out from amongst all the clutter. There, on a white enameled table, was a computer, two disk drives and a printer, an expensive combination of state-of-the-art equipment that, given the amount of research and writing she had left to complete for her section of the founding fathers' anthology, Emily would've given her eyeteeth to own.

But could she afford to buy such expensive equipment to complete her volunteer project more efficiently? Not on your tintype! she groused silently. Whereas, it appeared that Zachary Petty could indulge each and every one of his slightest little whims.

"This is your idea of a deep dark secret?" she scoffed, unable to keep an edge of sarcasm out of her voice. "You're some kind of a video-game fanatic?"

Zack shot her a withering glare, no longer willing to play along with her frequent intimations that his intellect was somehow inferior to hers. "After that crack, I'm not so sure you deserve to be told what I've been doing," he informed her coldly. "From what you said to me this morning, I thought that you'd readjusted your thinking concerning my intelligence, but apparently I was wrong."

Ashamed of herself for immediately jumping to the same wrong conclusion about him, especially when she knew that her sarcasm had been prompted by envy, Emily quickly apologized. "I'm sorry, Zack, and you're not wrong. I realize that you're a highly intelligent man."

Zack's response was contemptuous and terse. "Right."

"I do," she insisted. "Which is why it's so embarrassing for me to admit, even given what I now know to be true about you, that I'd still rather not let go of my unfounded prejudices.''

Instead of placating him, her sheepish admittance made Zack look even more exasperated. ''Well, why in hell not?''

''Because the way you make me feel scares me to death,'' Emily replied honestly after several seconds of silence, acutely aware that making such a confession to a man who had to fight off willing women probably wasn't very wise, but also aware that she had to stop lying to herself. ''I know how stupid this must sound, but the only way I can maintain any kind of control over those feelings is by telling myself that nothing can possibly come of our relationship because you and I don't have anything in common.''

''Because I'm all brawn and no brain,'' Zack concluded stiffly.

''That's been a very comforting fantasy for me to cling to, yes,'' Emily admitted.

Zack studied her crestfallen expression for several seconds, then realized how much it had cost her to reveal the vulnerability she felt around him, and his features softened into an indulgent smile. ''I don't want to frighten you any more than you already are, Em, but I happen to think that we've got quite a number of things in common, beginning with the unsettling fact that I want you every bit as much as you want me. I want you when I go to sleep at night, and first thing when I get up in the morning and every minute in between.''

To Zack's amusement, Emily looked far more thrilled by his admittance than frightened. ''You do?''

"I do," Zack confirmed. "But I've got a few fears of my own to deal with and that's why I haven't pressed the issue any harder with you. I've reached the point in my life when I want more than great sex with a woman. I also want an honest relationship."

Emily had reached a point in her life when "great sex" sounded pretty terrific, but even if she was willing to compromise all her morals to go to bed with this man, she could hardly blame him for expecting her to behave like a fully consenting adult. It wasn't Zack's fault that she'd developed a giant crush on her humanities professor during her second semester in college or that the unscrupulous man had compensated her for the gift of her virginity by giving her an A in his course. It wasn't Zack's fault that her first sexual experience had been so disappointing that she'd never been tempted to try it again or that she still lacked the sophistication to talk frankly on the subject of sex. As far as he could tell, she was a mature woman and, therefore, shouldn't have any trouble being up-front with him.

"I'm sorry, Zack, but it's very difficult for me to be honest with you about what I want," she acknowledged, and even as she forced the embarrassing words out of her mouth, she could feel herself blushing. "I haven't... that is, there's never really been... what I mean is, I don't—"

Zack placed his hands around her shoulders and cut off her awkward stammering before she could finish telling him what he already knew. "I know you don't have a great deal of sexual experience. Your body tells me that every time I come near you," he informed her bluntly.

"Oh," Emily murmured, and tried to look away, but Zack wasn't through talking to her and his fervent gaze demanded her attention.

"I like knowing that about you, Em. I like it very much. It makes everything we do together seem new and special."

Emily admitted softly, "It *is* new and special to me."

"I know, and that's why I can't let you walk into this situation blind," he stated firmly. "*I'm* the one who's been holding back on you, Em, not the reverse, and I'd like to rectify that. If we're going to take this affair beyond the preliminary stages, I want you to really know who you're getting involved with, trust that you're able to see past the famous quarterback to the real man."

Suddenly Emily felt more confused than embarrassed. Brows furrowed, she glanced over at the computer terminal and then back at Zack. "And the man you really are has something to do with that computer?"

Zack reached down for her hand and drew her over to the table. "It's a word processor," he said, then picked up a thin stack of paper that was sitting next to the printer. "And this is the first chapter of the mystery novel I've been writing since I quit my job at WCLN."

"Since you . . . !" Emily's mouth dropped open in disbelief, then clamped shut as her stunned brain finally absorbed his ludicrous announcement. "Did I hear you right?'' she demanded through gritted teeth. ''Are you actually trying to tell me that instead of going off to the studio every morning, you've been coming out here?''

Zack nodded. ''For the past two weeks.''

''Writing,'' she repeated dumbly, as if the word was alien to her vocabulary. ''While I've been looking after Angela, you've been out here writing!''

''That's right.''

''A mystery.''

''I've always been fascinated by the possibility of creating the perfect crime.''

''And Aunt Ida knows about this?''

''Yes.''

''But neither one of you thought it was necessary to tell me?''

Considering the outraged expression on her face, Zack was no longer so sure that telling her the whole truth and nothing but the truth had been such a brilliant idea. He'd expected Emily to be a tad indignant when she found out he'd misled her, to be annoyed with him for taking unfair advantage of her kindness, but she looked ready to do him bodily harm. That being the case, before she gave in to the urge to start swinging, which her clenched fists told him she was very close to doing, he stepped out of range and spoke to her from behind the safety of a stack of packing boxes.

''Sitting down to write a book has been a dream of mine for a very long time, but I didn't dare tell you what I was doing because I was afraid you'd quit on me,'' he explained sheepishly. ''And I do need you,

Em, even if I am working at home. You know what Angel's like. If I tried to write with her around, she wouldn't let me ignore her long enough to compose a decent sentence.''

But it's perfectly all right for me to shelve my own dreams while you fulfill yours, Emily raged inwardly, swallowing her outburst because she realized that Zack didn't know she'd harbored a similar desire for as long as she could remember. Even her aunts weren't aware that she'd written several love stories or that she'd been working on a long historical novel for more than a year. No one knew of it because she didn't have enough confidence in her storytelling ability to share her amateur endeavors with anyone.

To her dismay, she also realized that no matter how badly she'd like to jump all over Zack for placing his creative needs ahead of hers, she still didn't possess enough courage to admit to him or anyone else that she was a frustrated writer, too. Obviously she still had quite a ways to go in her personal-improvement program and that realization made her even angrier.

Not with Zack, but with herself.

''Did you tell the people at the studio why you were getting out of broadcasting?'' she inquired, wondering if anyone had laughed at his secret desire to be a writer and, if so, how he and his colossal ego had dealt with that blow.

Zack assumed by her curious expression that she'd gotten over her initial anger and he was heartily relieved. ''Lucky for me, I didn't have to tell them. It turned out that I was the world's worst commentator and that was clear to everyone by the second day.

Since I hated the job from the moment I picked up a microphone, I couldn't have been happier when they agreed to let me out of my contract. If Ed Baxter hadn't seen the light, I still would've quit, but legally things could've gotten very complicated.''

"And now you're free to do exactly as you like," Emily concluded dully, still fighting a perverse desire to rage at him for her own sense of inadequacy.

Zack shot her a questioning look, not sure what to make of her hollow tone. "I'm free to finally give it my best try," he agreed, but Emily wasn't looking at him, and she continued avoiding his gaze even when he closed the space between them and placed a hand on her shoulder.

She was definitely shutting him out, and Zack felt a wellspring of childhood insecurities surge up inside him. It suddenly became even more imperative for him to know if Emily was able to appreciate the quiet cerebral side of his nature, or if she was like his parents, his ex-wife and ninety-nine percent of the rest of the American public, who were only interested in the accomplishments of his flamboyant physical side.

Voice taut, he demanded, "Which part of this is upsetting you more? The part about my wanting to be a writer, or the part about my writing without telling you?"

Emily's chin came up and her brown eyes collided with his blue ones. "I'm not upset," she denied, but could tell immediately that her denial didn't convince him. "Okay, okay, so I'm a tiny bit miffed," she snapped in frustration, which instantly proved to Zack that "miffed" didn't quite cover it.

"With me?" he persisted doggedly. "Or with this sneaky setup?"

Since she'd already admitted to herself that she was a yellow-bellied, chicken-livered goose who couldn't even verbalize her dreams, let alone act on them, Emily stayed true to her recreant side and promptly chose the coward's way out. "You didn't have to skulk through the bushes like this, Zachary," she chided petulantly. "If you'd told me how this had all come about, I would've understood."

Then, damning herself for spouting a philosophy that she had yet to master, she insisted, "I could never criticize another person for being true to himself. That's something all of us should try to do."

Zack accepted her words as if they'd come in answer to a prayer. "I was hoping you'd feel that way, Em," he confessed, giving her shoulder an affectionate squeeze. "And I'm sorry I didn't tell you about this before now, but trust like this comes hard for me."

"Trust?" Emily jerked her shoulder out of his grasp. "Wait a minute here. You didn't feel you could trust me! I thought the reason you kept your writing a secret was because you were afraid I'd quit babysitting. Isn't that what you just said?"

"Well, yes, I said that... but to be honest, that wasn't the only reason or the most important one," Zack replied uncomfortably, aware that admitting the truth to her was almost as difficult as it had been to admit it to himself. "You see, Em, as far back as I can remember, people have discouraged me from pursuing anything that wasn't tied to athletics. As you're so fond of reminding me, that's where I first became a shining star, and I learned very early on that everyone expects that star to keep right on shining. I was afraid that when you found out I was writing a novel you might . . .''

Emily stared at him as his voice trailed off. Seeing that the tips of his ears had gone quite red, she realized that this seemingly self-possessed man, the man she'd assumed had reached out of the cradle to grasp the whole world by the tail, was in actuality struggling with the same kind of insecurities as she was. ''You were afraid that I'd laugh at you!''

Since her incisive accusation was accompanied by a barely muffled giggle, Zack glared resentfully at her. ''Which as it turns out, you are!''

''No, I'm not,'' Emily retorted, but she was unable to suppress her smile. ''I'm laughing because I just found out that you, too, have human frailties.''

Zack didn't find anything funny in that conclusion and he deeply regretted sharing his private aspirations with her when she obviously found his disclosure just short of hilarious. Fool that he was, he'd begun to believe that Emily Hartcourt was a dream come true for him, but it seemed she had no more sensitivity than any of the other women he'd been attracted to in the past. ''Yeah, hearing that the flashy star quarterback would rather write silly stories than show off his expert throwing arm really puts some tarnish on the ol' shine, doesn't it?''

The instant that bitter question came out of his mouth, Emily stopped smiling, and she reached out to snatch hold of his arm before he could turn away from her. Considering the amount of time she'd spent fantasizing about publishing contracts, six-figure advances and finding her name on a bestseller list, she couldn't let him think that she'd belittle his dreams no matter how farfetched they might be.

"Wait, Zack! Please, let me explain. I never intended to hurt your feelings, or make fun of you," she apologized. "It's just that I found it so comforting to know that it isn't always so easy for you to spit in the eyes of your detractors, that being master of your own fate all the time isn't any easier for the great Zoomer Petty than it is for me."

That explanation didn't do much to erase the wounded look on Zack's face, and Emily felt awful for being the one who'd put it there. Even after her apology, it was plain that he still thought she was being condescending, and the only way she could think of to change that erroneous opinion was to expose her own innermost dreams. Taking a deep breath to shore up her meager courage, she finally broke down and confessed, "You see, Zack, the fact is that I've always wanted to be a writer, too, but I was so afraid people would laugh at my puny efforts that I haven't dared tell anyone I've already written several stories or that I'm working on a historical romance."

For several seconds Zack just stood there staring at her as if she'd just admitted to being Godzilla. Then he grinned widely and exclaimed, "You're kidding! You're writing a romance novel!"

Emily reacted to his incredulity just as defensively as he'd reacted to hers. "Why is that so hard for you to believe?" she demanded. "Romance is in a woman's nature, and no matter how repressed you think I am, I'm still a woman!''

Zack cocked one brow at her, both astonished and delighted by her vehemence. "Trust me, Em, I never once thought otherwise."

"And my desire to write a romance is no more odd than your choosing to write a mystery!"

As he gazed down into her flashing dark eyes and watched her poke at his chest with one indignant finger, Zack felt an almost overwhelming relief and an exhilarating joy. For a short while there, he'd had reason to doubt it, but Emily had just proved to him that he'd been right to place his trust in her, and that realization made him want to shout with laughter. Of course, he'd also just learned that when it came to revealing personal hopes and dreams to another person, laughter wasn't an appropriate response for the listener to make. Somehow he managed to control his elation, but he couldn't resist the urge to scoop Emily up in his arms and start twirling her around.

"None of your desires are odd, Miss Hartcourt," he informed her magnanimously, just before his mouth covered hers. "Especially not the romantic ones."

Emily parted her lips on a startled squeak, but the sound was muted beneath Zack's hot seeking mouth, and although she didn't know what had prompted his ardor, it didn't take very long before her arms were wrapped tightly around his neck and she was returning kiss for kiss. As she's already discovered, when she was in Zack's arms, all other practical considerations ceased to exist. When Zack's mouth was on hers, it no longer mattered if she was upset with him, or if he'd kissed countless other women before her. She forgot about the fact she wasn't his type, nor he hers. The only thing that mattered was her mind-shattering need for him to go on kissing her and caressing her, and—

"Zack!" she gasped as he strode purposefully through the doorway into the next room and lowered her pliant body onto a quilt-covered mattress. "This is a bed!"

"Smart deduction," he complimented hoarsely as he came down beside her, and then, before she could voice any further protest, he brushed the wispy curls from her nape and began trailing moist kisses down the side of her neck.

"Zack," Emily whispered as a shimmer of delicious tingles raced down her shoulders and spine.

"Hmm?" he murmured, sliding his hands up under her tank top and brushing aside the lace cups of her unclasped bra so that he could more fully explore the smooth satiny skin of her breasts.

"We're making love on a bed in broad daylight. And...and this room has no curtains!" she stammered in desperation, yet moaned in obvious pleasure when she felt his warm palms close over her fullness, his fingers contracting.

"Right you are, professor," he concurred, then stopped her from making any other superfluous comments concerning their forthcoming activities by pulling her top over her head and tossing it aside. While she recovered from the knowledge that he intended to have her naked from the waist up, he stripped off her bra, then proceeded to provide her with proof that actions sometimes spoke far better than words.

Emily moaned as his mouth took hers and his hands stroked her body from her breasts to her waist. His lips teased hers, his tongue probed, and Emily forgot all about her inhibitions and admitted him eagerly into the sweet darkness of her mouth. The kiss grew much deeper, drugging all her senses, and Emily didn't murmur a single protest when he unbuttoned his shirt. As he shrugged out of it, she pressed her palms hungrily against his warm bare chest, admiring the ripple of muscle as he tensed beneath her touch. She was enthralled by the sight and thoroughly delighted by his involuntary reaction to the slightest movement of her fingers. It encouraged her exploration to become even bolder, and her hands roved freely over his muscular torso, but when they strayed below his waist, Zack groaned and jerked away.

Startled, Emily stared up into his face and saw that his eyes were half-closed and his jaw tight. "Zack?" she whispered, desperately afraid they were no longer operating on the same wavelength.

She sat up, about to act on that fear by scrambling off the bed, but then she noticed that Zack was staring at her naked breasts, and his hot tortured gaze paralyzed her. His breathing sounded harsh, and then he whispered something that shattered all her doubts and filled her with a wondrous sense of feminine power. "Lord, woman, this has never happened to me before. We're still half-dressed, but I want you so much I'm shaking with it."

"I'm glad," Emily whispered, reveling in the knowledge that she could inspire such intense desire in any man, let alone an experienced man like Zack, but then she made the mistake of smiling, a feline self-satisfied smile, and he saw it.

In one swift motion, he took hold of her waist and dragged her back down on the mattress. "I'm glad you're glad," he murmured huskily as he swiftly divested them both of their remaining clothes. "But fair is fair, and now it's time to make sure you're in the same condition I am."

Emily gasped at the sensual challenge in his tone and then felt the strong hard length of Zack's naked body pressed against the entire length of hers, and a dancing fire of shivering sensation jolted through her. She felt a bit threatened when he pinned her legs beneath the weight of his thigh, but then he lowered his head to her breasts and she felt nothing but pleasure. At the first skillful stroke of his tongue, her breathing came faster, and by the time he drew one taut nipple into his mouth she was quivering from head to toe.

"Okay, Zack, we're even now," she pleaded desperately, agonizingly aware that he possessed the driving power she needed to assuage the violent surges of feverish energy that were fast consuming her. "I need you so much I'm trembling."

Zack's chuckle was low and sexy and supremely male. "And I've only just begun."

Emily caught her breath as his hands began a slow tantalizing journey down her body, caressing the smooth flesh over her hips and across her bottom. His warm palms skimmed her bare stomach, then he parted her thighs, and his fingers found the heart of her desire. "Oh, please," she moaned in helpless abandon, but the pleasure kept building. Zack kept her exquisite torment at a fever pitch, driving her to the very edge of reason with nothing more than his expert touch.

The moans that came from far back in her throat were elemental cries of need, and Zack reacted to them fiercely, "That's it, sweetheart," he encouraged, as he swept her beneath him. "Give me all that fire."

As if trying to absorb him into herself, Emily arched her hips and clutched at him. More than happy to comply with her instinctive urging, Zack slid into her with one sure thrust. Her soft cry of satisfaction tore the air from his lungs, then her hands stroked down to his buttocks, pulling him deeper inside her. His heart began pounding, the hot pulses of wanting rushing heat through his body like a fire storm. He knew they'd been moving toward this moment from the first day they'd met, but even knowing that their lovemaking was inevitable hadn't prepared him for the reality.

Being inside her like this was sweet, hot, exquisite torture. He felt her softness opening to him, then clench tightly around him, and the fire of wanting her burned even hotter. Her hands were like liquid fire on his skin, fluttering over his shoulders and chest, dancing down his spine. Everywhere she touched him, he burned for her, and she caught his agonized rhythm easily, as if they'd made love countless times.

They were both caught up in the spiralling tension, but even in the midst of the storm, Emily was wildly delighted to discover that the mere touch of her hand, a seductive movement of her hips, added to Zack's pleasure. She opened her eyes to look at him as the coil tightened and saw that he was experiencing the same unbearable pleasure as she was feeling. Thrilled by that knowledge, she matched every one of his fierce movements, giving more and more of herself until, in a blinding flash of white heat and swirling colors, the coil snapped.

It seemed like forever before they were able to find anything tangible to cling to, but when Emily was finally able to focus again, she was aware that Zack was holding her with an almost bruising strength and that he was still locked deeply within her. He stirred slightly and it was as if she were still connected to some mysterious all-powerful force that, if aroused, could easily bring forth another storm.

To her amazement, as Zack shifted his legs, she felt a shocking renewal of heat and an equally shocking need to know if he felt it, too. Before either of them had fully recovered from the first tempest of sensation, she was inciting a second furor. She lifted her hips, twisting provocatively, anticipating the renewal of overwhelming pleasure, and before Zack realized what was happening to him, a tingling fire was licking along every one of his veins.

"Emily!" he gasped, but she was lost in the same haze rapidly overtaking him and was blind to everything else but need. Her eyes were closed, her head thrown back, and Zack smiled through his own hunger before surging upward, his urgency matching hers.

Release came with an explosion that was every bit as intense as the one that had preceded it, but Zack was the first to regain his senses. "I can hardly believe you could do that to me again so soon after the first time,'' he said jerkily, no longer sure if he'd been the seducer or the seduced.

Emily heard the disconcerted note in his voice, and her lashes fluttered open to find him staring down into her face. She was delighted by the incredulity she saw in a pair of irises that were still more green than blue, and aware that her sensual efforts were directly responsible for one color overtaking another, she smiled. ''As you said, Zack,'' she reminded him sweetly, ''fair is fair.''

Eight

As Emily sat down on the small gilt chair before her dressing table and reached for a bottle of her favorite scent, her eyes strayed to her bedroom window. It was going to be a beautiful night. The sky was clear, which meant that once the sun went down, the stars would be countless, and according to this morning's newspaper, there would be a full moon.

She shifted her gaze to the oak tree that grew in the side yard and could see the light from Zack's upstairs windows filtering through the leaves. Was he looking forward to this evening as much as she was? she wondered, but then her mutinous brain deviated to another far more troublesome question. Was Zack in as much danger of falling in love with her as she was with him?

"Oh, Lord," Emily breathed, and jerked her gaze away from the window. For the better part of the day, she'd consciously avoided the idea that she might be falling in love with Zachary, but another part of her was infused with a hopeless yearning, and that part was becoming harder and harder to fight. Her craving to be loved and wanted, to be held dear and cherished by someone, was growing stronger all the time. After making love with Zack, she'd not only started daydreaming about what it would be like to be married to him, but she'd also caught herself fantasizing over the possibility of bearing him a second child, a sister or brother for Angela, the little imp who had captured her heart even before the father had accomplished the same feat.

But, she reminded herself sternly, just because the fantasy seemed so wonderful didn't mean that Zachary Petty would leap at the chance to turn her idealistic dreams into reality. At this point in their relationship, beyond her ability to take care of his child until the nanny returned, all Zack wanted from her was terrific sex and an honest relationship, honesty being her ability to accept that other aspects of his life were much more important to him than his celebrity status.

"I can accept that but, oh, how I wish..." Emily glanced up at the fanciful woman who was staring back at her in the mirror. "Better nip that thought, lady," she warned. "Nip it in the bud! All you need to accept is that this affair is short-term, a brief romantic fling, and enjoy it while it lasts."

That said, she dabbed a drop of perfume behind each ear, tucked a rebellious strand of hair into the upswept style she'd chosen to wear for the evening and stood up from her dressing table. A second later, Esther walked into the bedroom, her gray eyes appearing more frigid than usual when she noticed that her niece's pale pink sari-style dress clung to her full breasts and left one shoulder completely bare. "So what Ida told me is true," she declared without preamble. "You're getting ready to go out somewhere with that man?"

"Yes, Zack invited me to dinner," Emily replied as she fastened a serpentine gold bracelet to her upper arm, then reached into her jewelry box for her matching earrings. "And he also mentioned something about going dancing afterward."

"Dinner and dancing," Esther echoed tautly as if those two harmless words had offended her ears most grievously. "So this isn't our local celebrity's idea of a gracious reward for a job well done, but something else entirely. You and Mr. Petty are going out on a date?"

"That's right," Emily confirmed, feeling the muscles in the back of her neck tighten as she prepared herself for the inevitable explosion.

When she spoke again, however, Esther's tone held far more concern than disapproval. "And it would also appear that you're greatly looking forward to the evening?"

"Yes, I am," Emily said in what she hoped was a matter-of-fact way, especially since she was aware that the tingling excitement she felt in every nerve ending wasn't caused only by her anticipation of sharing a candlelight dinner with Zack and dancing with him to some romantic melody, but by the knowledge of what was likely to happen afterward.

"I see," Esther stated thoughtfully.

Afraid that her aunt might see far too much if she noticed the dreamy expression on her face, Emily turned away from the mirror. If Esther Hartcourt ever suspected that her shameless niece had put the cart ahead of the horse, had made love with a man before conducting a single one of the normal courting rituals, there would be hell to pay, and Emily didn't want to hear any lectures on her lack of moral discretion. For once in her dull well-ordered life, she was going to follow her heart instead of her head. For once she was going to throw all caution to the winds, live solely for the moment and stave off any thoughts about the possible consequences of her reckless behavior.

"I certainly hope he likes this dress," Emily murmured absently to herself as she walked over to the bed and picked up her beaded evening bag and white silk shawl.

For some reason Emily couldn't comprehend, her innocent comment induced her aunt to come to a completely outrageous conclusion. "Why, Emily Anne Hartcourt, you've fallen in love!"

"What!" Emily cried in shocking consternation. "How on earth could you think something like that? After all, this is only our first date, and we certainly haven't reached the stage—"

Interrupting with a perfect rendition of her younger sister's favorite exclamation, Esther declared,

"Horsefeathers! Love doesn't follow any kind of schedule!"

"Well...no...but...uh...that still doesn't mean—"

Esther halted Emily's stammering with an impatient snort. "All that dithering only proves my point. Whatever stage you'd prefer me to think the two of you are at, the truth of the matter is right there on your face for anyone to see. You, my dear girl, are head over heels in love with Zachary Petty."

Her aunt's knowing tone set off a blistering heat in Emily's cheeks, and she silently cursed her body for betraying her. Even so, she still attempted to deny the depth of her feelings for Zack, because confronting that truth was pointless. "Really, Aunt Esther, I . . . I don't see how you could possibly—"

"My dear girl, I realize you think I wouldn't recognize love if it came up and bit me in the face," Esther admonished tartly as she took two steps back, then settled herself on the edge of Emily's bed. "But even a wizened-up old spinster like myself has some understanding of how it feels to fall in love. Believe it or not, I've experienced the emotion a time or two myself, and I've no doubt I looked every bit as starry-eyed as you do now. Just because none of my affairs of the heart never developed into anything permanent doesn't mean I have no understanding of what you're going through. Indeed, there was one young man, bless his soul, who could make me go weak in the knees with only a glance."

"That would be William Sherwood," Ida announced sagely as she bustled through the door,

stepped lightly over the worn spots in the frayed car-
peting, then perched herself on the bed next to her
sister. "As they liked to say back in my heyday, that
man was the cat's meow. Of course, he was only pass-
ably good-looking in comparison to his cousin John.
Now, that blue-eyed young devil was the catch of the
century."

"Both handsome and rich," Esther confirmed with
a sentimental smile that took years off her age. "But
I wouldn't have traded what I had with my Billy for all
the money in the world."

"Just because your Billy knew all the words to Lord
Byron's poetry didn't make him any more romantic
than my Johnny."

Emily listened in growing astonishment as the two
older women bickered back and forth over which one
of them had attracted the finer beau, and eventually
it became quite clear that neither of these affairs had
been platonic. "If you two were so much in love with
those men, why didn't either of you ever marry?" she
demanded when she was finally afforded the opportunity to get a word in edgewise. "Was keeping your
infernal independence really that important to you?"

Ida's brows shot up at Emily's impatient question,
then furrowed purposefully as she stared in her sister's direction. "Well, Esther?"

"If given the choice, we surely would have married, my dear. Unfortunately the war took that choice
away from us," Esther replied softly, her gray eyes
tearing up with what Emily suspected was an oft-
remembered pain. "Those two glorious boys fell to-

gether on D day, trying to secure a beachhead in Normandy.''

Ida sighed wistfully as she always did at the sad ending to that story, then reached out and patted her sister's hand before she turned her attention back to her niece. ''Which is why we're trying to advise you to reach out and grab whatever happiness you can, while you can. Time passes so quickly, Emily. If Esther and I have learned anything at all over the years, it's that none of us can afford to waste a single minute of it.''

To Emily's amazement, her straitlaced stodgy Aunt Esther promptly concurred with that philosophy. ''That's right, my dear. For some of us, there is no future beyond the present moment, so we must cherish each and every one we're lucky enough to be given. Ida and I may have loved and lost, but in the process of loving and losing, we also created some incredibly beautiful memories.''

''And it's time you created some of your own,'' Ida declared staunchly.

Esther nodded. ''Indeed it is. High time, I'd say. By thirty, I'd already cut quite a swath through the eligible male population.''

''No wider swath than the one I cut,'' Ida reminded her smugly.

''I'm speaking of quality, here, sister,'' Esther retorted. ''Not quantity.''

Emily stared at both women as if she'd never seen either one of them before. ''Am I hearing this right? Or have I suddenly gone crazy? Aren't you the same two people who condemned my mother for following her heart and running off with the man she loved? The same two who told me over and over again that a woman can't rely on a man for happiness? That she should never give up her independence?"

Esther's tone was dismissive, and she made a sweeping gesture with one arm as if she could wipe away three decades of dire warnings with a few comments. "At seventeen, your mother wasn't old enough to know her own mind. She was a naive, spoiled, selfish child who had absolutely no conception of what an adult relationship truly involved. Of course we could never approve of what she did."

"Or allow such a thing to happen to you," Ida clarified pointedly. "Since we were the ones most responsible for spoiling her."

"Yes, we were," Esther acknowledged somberly. "She was our darling baby sister, and we both adored her from the moment she was born, but I'm the first to admit I was the worst when it came to spoiling her. After our parents died, I made sure that Elaine always got anything she wanted, so it wasn't any wonder that she grew up relying on others to secure her own happiness. Unfortunately, when she fell in love with Roger Sims, she foolishly assumed that he would continue providing for her every need just as I had always done in the past, but he was no better equipped to survive in the cold cruel world than she was."

"Neither one of them had any idea what true independence really means," Ida explained. "They lived off Elaine's trust fund for the first few years, but when the money ran out, neither of them had any marketable skills to fall back on, and they soon learned they couldn't live on love."

Esther sighed. "And Roger quickly stopped pretending he could. When Elaine fell ill, he was already pursuing another wealthy young heiress, and within a few days after Elaine's death, he dropped you off with us so he could continue that pursuit unencumbered."

At long last, Emily was finally learning why her aunts, especially Esther, had been so fearful concerning her future and why they'd placed so much stress on her attaining a higher education. She only wished she'd understood their motivations long before now. That desire must have been clearly evident on her face for Esther murmured, "Maybe we should have explained all this to you when you were younger, Emily, but even now, it's very painful for me to speak about that tragic time. I loved your mother very much and blame myself for what eventually happened to her."

"And that's why she was so determined to make certain that nothing similar would ever happen to you," Ida nodded, but for Emily, further explanations were unnecessary. With one glance at the small picture that stood on her bureau, she understood everything.

"Even as a little girl, I looked just like her, didn't I?" she inquired gently.

"And you still do," Esther acknowledged, casting Emily the most affectionate smile she'd ever seen the woman bestow on anyone. "But unlike your mother, who never matured beyond childhood, you've become your own woman, Emily."

"A very fine caring woman," Ida clarified firmly. "Who can stand up on her own two feet and make sound decisions without the help of two interfering old biddies."

Esther rolled her eyes, but Emily noticed she was still smiling when she nodded her regal head and declared, "Indeed."

The doorbell rang precisely at seven, and Zack smiled in relief as he pulled open the door to admit his last-minute baby-sitter. "Glad you could make it, buddy," he greeted, shaking his head when he noticed that Brian "Boom Boom" Taylor had dyed half his hair again, and this time it was a glowing yellow.

Noting where Zack's eyes were centered, Brian laughed. "I got a photo shoot tomorrow at Dealin' Don's Used Cars," he explained with a gap-toothed grin. "They wanted my head to match that racing stripe on their logo."

"Classy touch," Zack commented dryly.

"Classy outfit," Brian retorted as he sauntered ahead of Zack into the great room. "They're paying me an insane amount of money to take a sledgehammer to an '83 Plymouth Duster. So where's the kid?"

Zack pointed to Brian's favorite room, then followed him into the kitchen. "Yo, Angel, I hope you've got plenty of my 'faborites' in that stash," Brian said when he spotted the toddler who was already dressed in her pj's and was now thoroughly occupied with the task of stacking a variety of bags onto the counter. "'Cus just between you and me, girl, I think your daddy's gonna be out all night makin' whoopee with some hot babe."

"Freebos!" Angela exclaimed triumphantly, and raced toward Brian, holding up an extra-large bag of corn chips, which the big man snatched up into his arms as effortlessly as he did the child.

Zack shot an uncomfortable glance at the line of open windows that faced Hartcourt House, hoping his friend's voice hadn't carried. Even though he knew no one was likely to be standing outside eavesdropping, he lowered his own voice another notch, just on the off chance that Ida was doing a little after-hours weeding in her herb garden. "Now that you mention it, Brian, can you handle it if I stayed out all night, or do you have to be at Dealer Don's real early in the morning?"

It wasn't often that Boom Boom Taylor was knocked off balance, but Zack's question staggered him. "You mean it!" he exclaimed, openmouthed. "We're talking about real live romance here? You're not just escorting some high-society type to help out a needy charity? Or paying off a favor to one of your buddies who's got an ugly sister or wallflower cousin just dying to meet the famous Zoomer?"

Zack scowled at him. "I have been known to take a woman out on a legitimate date occasionally."

"Sorry, bro, but I don't think two dates in one year qualifies as occasionally," Brian replied. "I know some married guys who have seen a hell of a lot more action than you."

Zack picked up his tan suit coat from the back of a kitchen chair and shrugged into it before he started walking out of the kitchen. "Okay, so maybe I've gotten sort of choosy about the kind of women I go out with."

"Aha!" his friend exclaimed, hoisting Angela onto one massive shoulder, then ducking so that she wouldn't bang her head on the top of the door frame as they followed her dad.

"Aha, what?" Zack demanded, shooting an annoyed glance over his shoulder.

Brian set Angela down on the couch and waited until Zack had inserted one of her kiddie movies into the VCR before replying, "You've got the hots for that old-maid schoolteacher next door, don'tcha, Zack? That sharp tongue of hers appeals to your scholarly mind?"

Sometimes Zack was amazed by how well his friend could read him and other times the man's uncanny perception irritated the devil out of him. "That's not the only thing about her that appeals to me, and Emily isn't an old maid," he said, unable to let that kind of remark pass without comment, even though he knew his defensive reply was as good as a confirmation. "She's four years younger than I am and not only the nicest, but one of the most beautiful, women I've ever had the pleasure of knowing."

Brian slapped his forehead. "I knew it! As soon as I met her I knew that haughty attitude would get under your skin. Straight off I could tell that football players didn't come up very high on her list, but all that did was prickle your interest, huh?"

"Yeah," Zack admitted. "It was nice to finally meet a woman who could look at me without seeing dollar signs and a bright future as my costar in those damned underwear commercials, which I'm beginning to think might never stop running.''

Brian laughed. "I'll bet our prickly Miss Hartcourt took one look at you and was so underwhelmed that it was all you could do not to throw her down and ravish her right there on the spot."

Zack's lips twitched. "Let's just say it's not my underwear or my talents as a quarterback that impress her."

Showing an agility that belied his mammoth size, Brian leapt over the coffee table and clapped Zack on the back. "Congratulations, buddy."

"For what?"

"For putting yourself back in the game. I was beginning to think that after your nasty experience with Shirley you were going to sit on the bench for the rest of your life, and that possibility had me real worried."

Zack still didn't like talking about that dark period of his life, but Brian Taylor had been a loyal friend to him throughout and Zack owed him a debt he could never repay. The big man had stayed by his side during all those painful weeks preceding his nasty divorce, and he'd still been there on the day the court had awarded custody of Angela to his ex-wife. The night Zack drank too much and flew into an irrational rage at a sleazy tavern in the worst part of town, it was Brian who'd prevented a gang of offended truckers from pounding the stuffing out of him. And later that night Brian was the one who'd layed a comforting hand on his shoulder while he'd cried like a baby.

"C'mon, Brian, you know a guy can't stay on the injured reserve list forever," Zack teased. "If you try getting any more mileage out of that leg, Coach Williams will kick your butt from here to Sunday."

The big man grinned at the picture Zack's words brought to mind. "If I'd have known that all a woman had to do to break through that wall you build up around yourself was give *you* a good swift kick in the butt, I would've sent Zena over here months ago. She's small, but let me tell you, that gal packs a mighty mean wallop. If you want, I could ask her to come over here and pull a few handfuls of hair out of your head. She's an expert at that."

Reaching up, Brian patted his half-bald pate. "And you've got much more of it to lose than I do."

"Forget it," Zack growled with a sympathetic chuckle. "You deal with your woman, and I'll deal with mine."

Brian's dark brown eyes twinkled merrily and he lifted one arm, laughing out loud when Zack's arm came up to meet his and they exchanged an exuberant high five. "Go for it, bro," Brian declared jovially. "As I always say, when it comes to feisty women, it's every man for himself."

When the knock came at the front door, Emily's stomach dropped to her toes, and she chided herself for feeling as giddy as a teenager going out with a boy for the very first time. Then when she remembered that, with one disillusioning exception and another soul-shattering one, her experience with the opposite sex hadn't progressed much beyond the kissing stage, she realized that a cure for the adolescent jitters didn't automatically come with age. Of course she was nervous. She was going out with a man who had advanced beyond the kissing stage aeons ago, and had every intention of advancing far beyond it with her again as soon as he'd given her a nice dinner and whirled her around the dance floor a few times.

That knowledge made Emily feel shaky all over, and her fingers were trembling so badly that it took two tries before she could attain a firm grasp on the doorknob. She finally managed to get the door open to admit Zack, but then she heard the soft whistle he emitted through his teeth, saw the green fire that ignited in his eyes as they traveled slowly down her silk-clad body, and her mouth went dry.

"You look utterly delectable," he said hoarsely. "So much so that we'd better get out of here before I decide to forgo dinner and eat you up instead."

A delicious tingle coursed down Emily's spine as he took her shawl and stepped behind her to drop it over her shoulders. His warm hands remained where they were overlong, and she couldn't seem to draw a normal breath or find the strength to move. "You look pretty good yourself," she managed as he finally moved back into place beside her and she conducted her own appraisal. "Navy blue is definitely your best color."

Zack chuckled. "A suit's a suit, but I'm glad you approve."

Emily had never been good at making small talk, but she did her best, asking him which restaurant they were going to try, what kind of food he preferred to eat and how he liked the fine weather they were enjoying. Unfortunately, by the time he'd gotten her settled comfortably in the passenger seat of his Jensen-Healey and had started the powerful engine, she'd run out of subjects to talk about. Then, just to leave him in no doubt that he had a bundle of quivering feminine nerves on his hands, when Zack attempted to instigate some conversation, she jumped like a scalded cat.

"Take it easy, sweetheart," he suggested silkily, and the knowing smile that accompanied the suggestion didn't soothe Emily's agitation one whit. "I don't plan to bite you—at least not for a while."

Emily tried, but she couldn't quite stifle her soft moan, and Zack almost drove over a crab-apple tree as he pulled away from the curb.

"I think we'd better make some last-minute adjustments in the schedule," he observed harshly, as he jammed the car into second gear and they sped off down the street. "What do you think?"

Since the only part of tonight's schedule that Emily couldn't stop thinking about took place on a bed, whatever they chose to do or not do beforehand seemed unimportant, and that being the case, she was happy for him to make all the decisions. "If you'd rather go somewhere other than Manley's, that's fine with me.'

"What I'd rather do is make love to you until our bodies are so relaxed and sated that keeping our food down won't be a problem," Zack replied, and when Emily jerked her startled gaze in his direction, she could see by his taut jaw and clenched hands that he was in the same strung-out condition she was.

That realization acted as a soothing balm to her agitated nerves, and suddenly Emily regained some measure of her scattered control. Of course, Zack couldn't see her inward smile, so he didn't realize that she was faking her appalled tone. "Zachary Petty! Are you suggesting that we bypass dinner and go have a quickie in some sleazy hotel?"

Zack released a long unsteady breath, then drew in another before he turned to her with a penitent expression on his face and admitted sheepishly, "Actually I was thinking of a long leisurely romp in a luxurious suite at the Lancaster in Capital Square."

Emily responded to that information in a prim-sounding voice, but there was a most unladylike gleam in her eyes. "Well, in that case, of course, I agree. A long leisurely romp sounds perfectly lovely."

"It does?" Zack exclaimed incredulously, then swallowed hard when he glanced over her and saw that she was eating him up with her gaze.

"Yes, indeed," Emily replied. "I don't know about you, but I'd hate for our first date to start out with the two of us getting sick all over the dinner table."

"I agree. That would put quite a damper on the evening," Zack confirmed, then stamped down hard on the accelerator.

"You don't have to speed, Zack," Emily admonished him sternly, then added in a sultry tone that made Zack feel as if he were about to explode. "After all, it's early yet, so we've still got several hours left to enjoy ourselves."

"Did I happen to mention that Angela's sitter is staying over?"

"Then we've got the whole night ahead of us," Emily murmured seductively.

"Oh, Lord," Zack groaned as if he were in acute agony. Emily's responsive laugh was filled with sweet feminine gratification as she settled down in her seat to enjoy the ride.

Nine

In deference to Emily's unpredictable sense of propriety, Zack bypassed the curved drive in front of the hotel and found a parking place in an empty lot that was almost a full block away from the busy entrance. They didn't have any luggage, and although he'd bet money that the hotel's well-trained doorman wouldn't raise an eyebrow over that telling lack, he didn't want Emily to suffer the slightest twinge of embarrassment when they checked in and thereby decide to change her mind. With a determined stride, he walked around the rear of the car, opened the door for her, then tucked her arm through his and led her purposefully onto the sidewalk.

As they strolled together down the night-darkened street, he kept one arm possessively around her waist. The warm glow shining down on them from the well-lit buildings facing the street was nothing compared to the flames that blazed hotter and hotter inside him with every step they took closer to the hotel. All the nerves in his body felt as if they were on fire, and if her rapid breathing was any indication, Zack suspected that the woman beside him was suffering from the same kind of heat.

Emily was definitely in an overheated condition, but ''suffering'' wasn't the word she would've used to describe her current state. ''Light-headed'' was a far better term. She was aware of Zack with every fiber of her being. The brush of his thigh against hers as they walked made her senses reel, and in order to maintain her balance, she was forced to slide her arm around his waist.

Zack immediately tightened his grip and bent his head to whisper in her ear. ''Tonight is ours, Em. All night.''

The air around them was laden with an intoxicating variety of smells. Traffic on the street was heavy, and several other couples were strolling along the avenue, but Emily was oblivious to everyone and everything but the handsome man beside her. ''Our night, all night,'' she promised softly in return, the quick tapping of her high heels on the concrete pavement setting a cadence that urged them both to quicken their pace.

It was as if they were connected by some invisible current of magnetic energy, a powerful force that obliterated all reservations and prevented even a fleeting instant of second thought. Emily was only dimly aware of passing through the hotel's revolving glass door or pausing at the front desk long enough for Zack to check them in. When the elevator whisked them upstairs to the twentieth floor, she felt as if she were floating, and as they walked down the carpeted hallway, it still seemed as if her feet weren't quite touching the ground.

With fingers that fumbled, Zack unlocked the door to their room and Emily preceded him into the darkened suite. She'd only gone a few steps before the lights came on and she was pulled back into a strong pair of arms.

"At last," Zack whispered, then lowered his head and crushed her lips beneath his.

Emily melted into his embrace, heady with the sensual delight of his assaulting tongue tantalizing the interior of her mouth. Her arms wound around his neck and her fingers winnowed through the thick golden hair at the back of his head. Her flimsy shawl slithered from her shoulders, falling silently to the floor, and Zack smoothed his fingertips along her bare skin until he found the delicate catch at her nape. Then, with a jerky impatient motion, he tugged down the zipper, exposing the full length of her slender back to his questing touch.

"I want you, woman," he growled hungrily. "I'm dying for the taste of you."

Emily was still trying to recover her breath after that first heart-stopping kiss when his lips came down on hers again and his tongue plunged into the sweet moist interior of her mouth. She moaned her delight as he tasted his fill and moaned again when his hungry lips moved away from her mouth to savor the flavor of her skin. As if starving, Zack kissed her cheek, her chin, the soft skin below her earlobe, then he nibbled his way down the sensitive cord at the side of her neck.

At the feel of his teeth grazing the width of her naked shoulder, Emily arched against him, gasping in pleasure when his large hands cupped her firm rounded bottom and he brought her lower body into searing contact with the tangible evidence of his desire. "Make love to me, Zack," she whispered frantically. "Now. Take me now."

Instantly his hands swept down her trembling body, stripping away the pink silk dress and the strapless French lace bra beneath it, leaving her with nothing on but her panties. Then he scooped her up in his arms and carried her to the king-size bed, his mouth leaving hers reluctantly as he pulled back the heavy quilted spread and laid her down on cool satin sheets. Emily gazed up at him, her eyes almost black with the intensity of her longing as he stripped off his coat, tie and shirt. Then, holding her fascinated eyes prisoner with the devouring passion in his flaming gaze, he slowly unbuckled his belt and stepped out of his trousers.

In a desire-laden trance, Emily reached up with both arms, basking in the heated depths of his darkened eyes as he gazed down at her. "Just looking at you makes me ache," he whispered, staring at the beautiful breasts he'd recently uncovered, then dragging his appreciative eyes away from that glorious sight to survey the other bountiful female treasures that would soon be within his clutches. The longer he looked, the more he ached, until he couldn't restrain himself any longer.

Emily held her breath as Zack reached down to her, inserted one finger beneath the elastic waist of her panties and drew them slowly over her legs. Then, his eyes never leaving hers, he lowered himself onto the bed and moved his body completely over hers. She felt the blatant maleness of it, the heat, the tickle of hair against her aroused breasts and his exquisite weight. Her hungry eyes looked straight back into his as he pressed his lips against her softness.

"I love how this feels," she whispered, her hands running over his long broad back. "I love how you feel."

Zack's breath grew increasingly rapid and heavy as she continued her tactile exploration of him and he matched her touch for touch until each ardent caress became pure torture. Zack fit his body between her thighs and his mouth descended on hers, the probing insistence of his tongue parting her lips easily.

Emily moaned in shameless pleasure, fitting herself more closely against him as she responded to the hungry demand of his exploring hands and tongue. His heated skin slid down her body and his mouth left hers to begin a seemingly endless journey across her breasts. He breathed flame around her hardened throbbing nipples, and his fingers traced lower, setting off depth charges of delight as they caressed the very core of her. Driven mindless with the need for release from the overpowering tension, Emily arched higher against him, begging him for the feel of his bold masculinity within her soft flesh.

Zack complied with that urgent appeal with one smooth thrust, then set a rocking rhythm within her that she followed eagerly. The surging male power of him filled her, sending her even higher, and Emily wrapped her legs around his, taking him with her into those vast steamy clouds of sensation. Together they rose, soaring closer and closer to the wondrous explosion they had each set off in the other, and when it came, they endured that together, too.

For a long time they lay entwined, spent and joined in some new intangible way. Neither was willing to relinquish the other and when at last they were forced to make concessions for the sake of comfort, it was only to turn onto their sides and adjust their embrace. Emily gazed into the sated glow on Zack's face and smiled, memorizing his expression for her memory book. At long last, one of her most cherished adolescent fantasies had come true. She, a straight-A student, member of the National Honor Society and captain of the debating team, had captured the eye of the handsome star football player and had given him one of the most memorable nights of his life.

Seeing her complacent smile, Zack kissed the tip of her nose and closed his eyes, capturing the sensual luminance of her expression, the deep splendor in her liquid dark gaze, and holding it inside him like a winner's trophy as he waited for his labored breathing to return to normal. Unfortunately he never was able to fully recover his breath. He couldn't seem to stop touching her, his hands gliding over her satiny skin gently, compulsively.

Emily could find no fault with that. She cuddled even closer to him, wanting only to remain near him, touching him, feeling his arms around her and his heart beating steadily beneath her cheek. She closed her eyes to savor every feeling, every moment.

She had never felt such a strong sense of security before, this kind of total peace. She felt at home in his arms, but soon the home fires were blazing out of control once more. Her lashes fluttered open to find the rekindled glow in Zack's eyes, and she was instantly ready to walk through the flames with him again.

Over the next two hours, they behaved like longtime lovers. They delighted in one another's bodies, whispered soft sexy messages into one another's ears, teased and tickled. Eventually Zack convinced Emily that they should take a shower together, and beneath the spray of warm water, Emily gathered more beautiful memories into her heart, thrilling mementos she would take with her to her grave.

It was midnight before Zack decided they were finally relaxed enough to order room service, and when their tray came, they placed it between them on the wide bed and made love to each other with their eyes, while they devoured a bowl of luscious fruit, drank champagne and fed each other small delicious bites of ham, pressed turkey and aged cheddar cheese. Neither one of them had any trouble digesting their midnight feast, a fact that Zack pointed out before he placed the empty tray on the floor.

When he rolled over again onto his back and turned his head on the pillow to look at her, he was pleased to notice that their long luxurious romp between the sheets hadn't diminished her lustful interest in his body. "Wanna dance?" he inquired huskily.

Emily glanced down at her bare breasts and thighs, then over at his equally naked form, sprawled out in magnificent splendor on the opposite side of the bed. "Sorry, but I can't seem to find the energy to move, let alone get up and put clothes on."

Zack issued a replete sigh. "Me, neither, but I did promise you dinner and dancing and I don't want you thinking I don't deliver on my promises."

"You're extremely generous in other ways," Emily informed him with a naughty giggle. "I have absolutely no complaints."

"Me, neither," Zack returned with a warm smile as he reached down to pull the sheets up over them both, then settled back with a contented sigh amongst the soft pillows. "So how long do you think we should wait before we get married?"

Emily's heart stopped beating for several moments as a boundless joy expanded in her chest, but then her traitorous brain started relaying images of their recent lovemaking, recalled for her delectation every erotic syllable he'd spoken to her over the past few hours, every husky murmur and hoarse whisper. Not once, at any time, had he mentioned the one word that Emily considered absolutely essential, and the absence of it diminished her joy, kept her from flinging herself across the bed and crying, *I love you... I love you... I love you!*

"Married?" she said warily. "Why would you want to marry me?"

Zack laughed and lifted an amused eyebrow at her. "Considering what we've been doing with each other for the better part of today, I would think that would be obvious.''

''Not to me,'' Emily ventured, praying for him to give her the words, willing him to say them. *I love you, Emily. I love you so much that I can't bear the thought of living any longer without you by my side.*

Instead, Zack issued an impatient sigh, shoved himself up in the bed until his shoulders were resting against the headboard and began ticking off practical reasons for matrimony on his fingers. ''Number one, Angela needs a mother and she adores you. Two, unlike my first wife who was less enamored with me than with the glamorous life-style I led, you would prefer staying home with me in our nice big house, on our quiet street, where our children, lots of normal happy children, could enjoy a happy normal childhood. Three, we're extremely compatible in bed and after tonight's marathon, I can almost guarantee that we'll remain so for the rest of our lives. And four....''

Zack paused and Emily mentally crossed her fingers praying that his next words would be that they were kindred spirits, that along with his own expectations, he would include some of her personal dreams for the future in his outline for their marriage, but her prayers were in vain.

Zack cast her a playful look before concluding, ''You're the only woman I know who's smart enough to keep up with the brilliant likes of me.''

Emily was also smart enough to figure out that he didn't love her. He desired her body, yes, admired her intellect, but what he was truly in love with was the idea of having a well-established home, a contented wife and a mother for his children. She couldn't blame him for wanting those things. She embraced a similar dream, although her needs went far beyond his. Her dreams were based on an emotion Zack might never be capable of giving her, and she couldn't marry him without it.

Furthermore, she still had major problems with his self-centered approach to the world. He might claim otherwise, but he always expected everything to come out his own way and everyone around him to comply with his slightest wish. In Zack's mind, his desires would naturally be her own.

"So, is that enough to convince you to marry me, Em?" Zack demanded when she remained silent.

Emily sat up straight, pressing her body upright against the pillows as she dragged the sheet up to cover her breasts. "No, Zack, it isn't," she stated tartly. "To me, marriage is forever, and I'm not ready to make that kind of commitment to you."

Zack felt as if all the oxygen had suddenly been sucked out of his lungs, and for a few seconds, he couldn't breathe. Then when he was finally able to draw an agonized breath, his head started throbbing. He'd made a lot of arrogant assumptions in his life, but by the sounds of it, he'd really outdone himself this time.

From the very beginning of their relationship, he'd operated under the assumption that Emily was the kind of woman who wouldn't go to bed with a man unless she loved him, and that she'd expect a marriage proposal to follow fairly closely on the heels of lovemaking. Now, though he could still hardly be-

lieve what he was hearing, he was forced to acknowledge that she possessed a much more modern outlook
on male-female relationships than he did. Either that,
or she felt he was rushing her into a decision she wasn't
quite ready to make.

Was that her problem? Did Emily feel he was rushing her? Of course she did, Zack answered himself, for
if that wasn't the reason for her reservations, he would
have to admit he'd been totally wrong about her from
the very start, and he was almost certain that couldn't
be true. Emily Anne Hartcourt was an old-fashioned
girl with old-fashioned values, and all she was trying
to do was hold herself true to them.

"When do you think you'll be ready?" he inquired, willing to indulge her need for caution even if
he didn't share it.

Emily bit her lip, then shut her eyes and said what
needed to be said. "I'm not sure I'll ever be ready for
marriage. I'm very content with my life as it is. I already have a nice home and a fulfilling career,
and...and even though I adore Angela, I'm still not
sure I'd make her or anyone else a very good mother."

Aha! Zack exclaimed silently. Now, they were getting to the real heart of the matter, the underlying basis for Emily's fears, and he gave himself a mental pat
on the back for making the decision to indulge her.
"Well, I'm sure you'll be a great mother, Em," he as-
serted emphatically. "Where Angel's welfare is concerned, your maternal instincts have always been right
on target."

Emily was gratified by his faith in her, but even if
she turned out to be an excellent mother for Angela

and any other children they might have, that didn't mean she'd enjoy a similar success as Zack's wife. How could any wife be happy knowing her husband didn't love her?

"Maybe so," she allowed softly. "But parenthood aside, I believe that love has to precede marriage."

Zack's jaw felt as if it had been changed to granite. Did she love him or didn't she? All his instincts told him she did but she was telling him otherwise, and Emily Hartcourt wasn't the type to lie. Could he really have misread her this badly? "I see," he replied, though he was no longer sure he did.

Emily glanced over at Zack, then wished she hadn't, for the impact of his eyes boring into hers was devastating. "Do you?" she whispered, fearing he couldn't see anything through the red haze of smoke rising from the wound she'd just dealt his ego. "Do you see that what we have together isn't enough to sustain a marriage?"

"Let's forget about what I see, Emily, and concentrate on what you're missing!" Zack retorted.

Placing both hands on her shoulders, he twisted her upper body around to face him. He gave her a little shake. Then acting on the premise that she couldn't possibly give herself so completely without loving him, he demanded, "Can you deny that I can make you want me so much it hurts? Can you?"

"That's not the point—" Emily began, but the rest of her words were cut off abruptly when Zack pulled her down on the bed, then swept her body beneath his. With his eyes fastened on her parted lips and his demanding hardness pressing against her, her brain ceased to function and she was unable to form any words of denial.

Zack's lips took hers and Emily moaned helplessly, a sound that made him smile. Whatever she said, she was his. She would always be his.

"Oh, Zack, passion isn't love," she protested when he finally let her up for air. She wanted so badly to convince him of that, but he swiftly reminded her of the desperate need she had to hold him tightly against her, to feel the taut lines of his body merging with her own. Unable to deny that need, her arms came up to reclaim possession of him, clinging to his neck as she drew his mouth back down to hers.

Within seconds, she was aflame, her desire for him igniting as quickly as always. Her protesting speech was forgotten in their delirious exchange of drugged kisses. With Zack, she became a wild uninhibited creature incapable of holding back. With him, she could never give less than her all.

"Is this the feeling you're not ready for?" Zack demanded, as he cupped one breast in his palm, using his teeth, tongue and lips to increase the vibrating agony of anticipation. "Is it the loss of control you experience in my arms that scares you?"

"Lust isn't love," Emily whispered frantically. "Wanting isn't loving."

Zack wedged his knee between her thighs, pressed forward then relaxed, making her loins ache with renewed yearning. He was intent on inciting every nerve to the same fever pitch, ruthlessly determined to show her that her idealistic notions about sex, love and marriage didn't work in real life.

"Is this the kind of fulfillment you're willing to do without because it doesn't comply with your sophomoric definition of love?"

Zack's question and the disdainful tone in which it had been asked acted like a fire extinguisher, completely dousing the flames of Emily's desire. "Sophomoric!" she exclaimed irately, pushing him off her as she struggled to put as much space between them as possible. "What do you mean by that?"

Zack let her go and rolled off the bed, his expression as angry and upset as hers. With a savage motion of his arm, he scooped his trousers off the floor and pulled them on, then retrieved the rest of his clothes. "Sophomoric. A characteristic to describe a know-it-all person whose thinking is actually immature or foolish," he recited sarcastically, glaring at her as if she were an appallingly dim-witted student who'd just failed a simple vocabulary test.

"I understand what the word means," Emily retorted indignantly. "What I was asking is how you think it applies to my feelings about love. Is it foolish for a woman to want a hearts-and-flowers kind of romance?"

"You're not a teenager anymore, Emily, and neither am I. What we've just shared is all there is. If you want flowers I'll get you flowers, but do you honestly believe that kind of romantic nonsense will change how we feel about each other?"

"No, I don't," Emily replied bitterly, fighting back scalding tears. "But I do think it would be nice if there were other reasons for us to get married besides lust and the practical ones you listed with less than poetic flair.''

Zack paused in the act of buttoning his shirt to shoot her another scornful glance. ''Obviously you think love should be conducted on some higher ephemeral plane where gentlemen spout romantic poetry and ladies swoon, but courting rituals like that went out of fashion with the bustle. Sorry if this bursts your romantic bubble, lady, but if you plan on waiting around for a man who'll write you poetry, you'll be stuck alone in that ivory tower of yours for the rest of your born days.''

The only thing that Emily thought obvious was that Zack was spoiling for a fight, and she was equally anxious to give him one. With that defiant purpose in mind, she slid off the bed and stomped around the room in search of her discarded clothes, refusing to give him the advantage of conducting their argument while he was fully dressed and she was vulnerably naked. In smoldering silence, she struggled back into her underclothes and dress, then bent to pick up her high heels.

As he watched her jerky movements, heard the frustrated unladylike oath she muttered when her foot refused to slide gracefully back into her shoe, Zack admonished, ''Now, what that should tell you, Cinderella, is that fairy tales rarely work out perfectly in real life.''

''I don't need anyone to tell me that you're not Prince Charming,'' Emily retorted scathingly. ''Even with my fanciful little head stuck up in the clouds, I'm still able to figure that fact out for myself.''

"Oh, yeah?" Zack said, looking at her with such a sardonic expression on his face that Emily's temper instantly soared higher. "If you're so good at figuring, have you figured out yet how one and one can add up?"

At her blank expression, Zack growled, "Let me make it easy for you, professor. Without the use of birth control, the sum of one and one is often three."

Horrified, Emily stared at him, and all the color drained from her face. "Oh, my Lord!" she gasped. "I never thought... I never realized... Oh, for goodness' sake."

"Goodness has nothing to do with the fix you've put us in."

"Me!"

"Yes you! Up until tonight, everything you've ever said has led me to conclude that you were a traditional woman with old-fashioned values. If I had known that behind that prim front, you academic types embrace the Bohemian life-style where free love is the byword, I would've walked into this situation prepared. Instead, fool that I am, I made love to the woman I believed I was soon going to marry. So of course I didn't bother with any protection."

"Oh!" Emily looked around for something to throw at him. She'd never felt so close to violence in all her thirty years. To her dismay, there was nothing within reach that would do enough damage, so she had to content herself with a verbal assault.

"Isn't that just like you, Zachary Petty," she shrieked. "Macho man that you are, all you care about is satisfying your Neanderthal urges. Keep the little woman barefoot and pregnant. Isn't that how you arrogant jocks think?''

"So we're back to that again, are we? Now I get it.''

"Get what?''

Zack glared at her, his eyes as cold as an arctic sea. Then he started advancing on her slowly, menacingly, his gaze never leading her face.

Emily stood her ground valiantly, though every instinct told her she would be wise to run. No wonder he'd been considered the Cougars' most lethal weapon! The ruthless look in his eyes and the catlike grace with which he stalked her proved him to be the personification of the predatory beast his team had been named for. Tonight she was seeing a side of Zachary Petty she'd never seen before, but she was certain that those men who'd opposed him on the gridiron had been victims of it every Sunday afternoon.

When he came to a stop only inches from where she was standing, Emily braced herself for a physical assault. But then, in a deceptively quiet voice, he said, "Pardon me for being so slow on the uptake. I'm the one who's been a romantic fool. All you wanted out of this was a night in the sack with a muscle-bound stud, wasn't it?''

She flinched. He wasn't too far off base with that accusation. Before leaving the house this evening, hadn't that been exactly what she'd been willing to settle for? A hot passionate affair with a sexy hunk. If she was honest with herself, she had to admit she'd demonstrated no more scruples over the past few hours than any of the empty-headed bimbos who were constantly in pursuit of him.

Emily stared back at him wordlessly for several seconds, then, thoroughly intimidated by his sheer physical presence, she shrank within herself and stumbled backward. "I...I never expected a marriage proposal," she stammered. "An...an affair is all I thought you wanted."

"Well you thought wrong," Zack snarled, the force of his rage driving her quaking body into the closest chair. "I told you I was looking for an honest relationship with a woman. In my book, an honest relationship leads to marriage. It doesn't mean sneaking off to some hotel for a sleazy affair. From the very beginning, *my* intentions were honorable."

Unable to bear the condemnation in his eyes or withstand her own guilt, Emily dropped her stricken face into her hands. "Oh, Zack," she cried. "I don't know what to say."

Blinded to all but his own pain and rage, Zack countered brutally, "If you're at a loss for words now, lady, what are you going to say when you present your illegitimate child to the world?"

Ten

"No, I can't be pregnant," Emily whispered, staring blindly at the patterned carpet beneath her feet. But it took only a few mental calculations to cast a fair amount of doubt on that optimistic claim. Those doubts increased even more when her damning calculations were added to the number of times she and Zack had made love in the past twenty-four hours.

Reeling, she threw herself back against the cushions of the chair. No matter how she viewed the situation, conditions were perfect for conception and she'd done absolutely nothing to prevent it!

Zack had been right to say that fairy tales rarely worked out perfectly in real life, Emily realized morosely. But he'd been wrong to call her Cinderella. She had much more in common with Sleeping Beauty, a woman who'd been blind to all danger because she'd been cast under a spell.

Like that bewitched princess, Emily had been sheltered and protected for the greater part of her life by her fairy godmothers. In the hopes she'd avoid her own self-destruction, she'd been encouraged by them to keep herself safe in an ivory tower. But what had she done the minute she'd been released from her aunts' benevolent rule? She'd floated right up into the tower suite of the closest hotel and sealed her own fate. Princess Aurora had been lured to the castle tower by a siren's call, and her twentieth-century counterpart had been rendered just as mindless by the ancient call of passion.

"At least Aurora had the excuse of ignorance," Emily muttered under her breath. She, however, had no such excuse. Knowing full well how this evening was going to end, she still hadn't devoted one moment of thought to the biological ramifications of sex. She'd been so completely enraptured by the pleasure she experienced in Zack's arms that she'd lost all sense of responsibility.

Oblivious to Zack's presence, Emily straightened abruptly in the chair, acutely aware that the fates rarely allowed anyone to escape the consequences of their own recklessness. She'd danced all night to a wonderous tune, and now it was time to pay the piper. "Oh, Lord, I probably am pregnant."

Zack didn't think it was possible for him to get any more upset with her, but she'd just confirmed the plausibility of his worst-case scenario, and that did the trick. "Damn you," he swore. "This is your most fertile time, isn't it?"

"Yes," Emily agreed, too miserable to care if Zack launched into another angry tirade. "I'm a totally irresponsible idiot."

"Well, that makes two of us," Zack retorted wearily, though his willingness to shoulder part of the blame didn't make Emily feel any better or change her outlook on the future.

"No," she sighed fatalistically. "This is my problem, and I'll take full responsibility for it. You don't have to be involved at all."

Feeling as if he'd just taken a debilitating blow to the solar plexus, Zack dropped like a stone into the chair opposite hers. Then, taking a white-knuckled grip on the upholstered arms, he braced himself for the answer to his next question, no longer certain he could trust her to give him the right one. "Oh, really? And how do you intend to take care of the 'problem'?"

It didn't take a genius to figure out what Zack was truly asking, and Emily was repelled by the very thought of an abortion. Maybe Zack didn't love her, but she loved him, and if she bore his child, she'd always have a tiny part of him, to hold dear. No matter how he felt about her or their ill-fated relationship, Emily could only feel joy when she thought about having his child.

"If I'm pregnant, I have every intention of keeping my baby," she declared fiercely.

"It would be my baby, too," Zack reminded her just as fiercely. "And I *am* involved whether you like it or not. If you have my child, you're going to have to put up with me, too, because we'll come as a package deal.''

"Under the circumstances, I hardly think—'' Emily began.

Zack immediately cut her off, refusing to listen to any more of her misguided arguments. Coming up out of his chair, he loomed over her. "Let me make this perfectly clear. There will be no fight over who gets custody of this child,'' he informed her bluntly. "I've already been down that road once before and I'll never put myself or any child of mine through that kind of suffering again.''

Emily didn't want to face some long-drawn-out custody battle any more than he did, but she wasn't about to give up her baby. "What exactly are you implying?'' she demanded, needing to know just how far he intended to go with what sounded very much like a threat.

"I'm not implying anything. I'm telling you. I missed out on Angela's infancy because her mother won custody in our divorce. God only knows how much more of her life I might have missed out on if Shirley hadn't died, which is why I won't miss out on anything with any future child I might have.''

Zack's position was clear, but Emily felt just as strongly about hers. "I understand how difficult that must have been for you, Zack, but if it turns out that I really am pregnant, I won't let you take my baby away from me! If you try, I'll fight you tooth and nail! A baby needs its mother.''

Zack curled one hand over each armrest, then leaned forward to pin her in place with his steadfast gaze. "As I keep trying to tell you, there won't be any fight, Emily. Any child we might have will be raised by both its parents."

Emily gasped, as his meaning finally came clear to her. "Are…are you saying that you still want to marry me?"

"Want to? Maybe not," Zack admitted bitterly. "But if you're pregnant, I'm going to, and you'd better get used to that idea."

"How can I possibly get used to such a crazy idea?" Emily cried out in pain and frustration, pushing her palms against his chest until he allowed her to stand. "Getting married for the sake of the children makes even less sense to me than people who won't get divorced because of them."

"Maybe so, but that's what we're going to do," Zack countered. "If not, you can be the one to explain it all to Angela. Who knows? Maybe you'll even manage to convince her that you love her just as much as the new baby you're carrying. Of course, if you follow that up by walking out of her life, I can guarantee she won't believe you. Are you cruel enough to do that to her, Emily?"

Incensed that he could even think she'd do anything to hurt Angela, Emily exclaimed, "Of course not!"

The gleam of victory in his eyes, Zack smiled mirthlessly. "Then do I have your promise that if you're pregnant, you'll marry me?"

Emily's shoulders sagged in defeat. "I guess I have no choice."

"How soon will you know?"

"Three weeks ought to give me a strong clue."
Zack nodded. "So be it."

The following morning, Zack had opened the door
to find Emily standing on the doorstep, as per their
normal weekday schedule. "I didn't expect you to
come to work today," he'd admitted softly, noting the
dark shadows under her eyes and the abnormal pallor
of her skin. "I would've understood if you hadn't."

"Would Angela?" she'd inquired just as softly, not
waiting for an answer as, back straight and head held
high, she'd stepped around him.

Zack had remained where he was, a deep furrow
creasing his brows as he'd stared thoughtfully after
her, but Emily hadn't so much as glanced his way
again as she'd mounted the stairs to his daughter's
bedroom, and every day since then she'd avoided his
eyes. At first, he'd concluded that she felt so guilty for
deceiving him about the less than loving feelings she'd
had for him that she didn't have the guts to look him
in the eye, but by the end of the first week, he'd realized that courage wasn't something she lacked.

After that horrible argument they'd had at the hotel and all the nasty accusations he'd hurled at her,
Emily had still showed up bright and early every
morning prepared to live up to the letter of their em-
ployment agreement. Although it seemed to hurt her
to look at him, she was there for his daughter full-
time, making sure that Zack was given a complete
eight hours a day to work in the carriage house. Unfortunately Zack had been much too busy thinking
about her and her confusing behavior to do much

writing, and with each passing hour, his confusion increased.

When she wasn't aware he was in the house, Zack discovered that Emily acted just like the woman he'd fallen in love with, a sweet caring woman who stuck bandages on a little girl's imaginary cuts and made up lyrical ditties that Angela didn't even realize contained clever educational lessons. Wearing a smile that belied the wounded expression in her gaze only the most discerning eye could have noticed, Emily read his daughter stories, played games, baked cookies and answered thousands of how comes and whys.

Not too long ago, Emily had revealed the fact that she was a frustrated writer, also, yet she'd never once complained to him about the lack of time she'd recently been given to devote to that occupation. As far as he could tell, she was always putting someone else's needs above her own. When she wasn't doing something nice for Angela or himself, she was doing something for her aunts or other people. Recently Ida had disclosed the information that Emily was also working on a Founders' Day project for the local historical society, which told him that even the community at large felt free to make demands on her time.

Whenever he thought about her selfless behavior, Zack found himself asking the same troubling question. Would such a kind generous woman really get involved with a man only to gratify a passing lust? The answer he kept coming up with to that question was a resounding *no!* Day in and day out, Emily was simply Emily, and no matter what she'd said to him that fateful night in their hotel room, she'd obviously lied to cover up her real reason for refusing to marry him. But what could that reason possibly be? And why didn't she feel she could tell him the truth?

Leaning back in the swivel chair in front of his computer, Zack tried to recall the exact words Emily had used to him that night. *Is it so wrong for a woman to want a hearts-and-flowers kind of romance?... Passion isn't love... Wanting isn't loving... Love has to precede marriage.*

Zack sighed. Like it or not, everything she'd said still boiled down to the same thing. Emily didn't love him.

Then, as he continued to stare despondently at the blank screen of his word processor, Zack was hit by a possibility that had never occurred to him before and his mouth dropped open. "*She* doesn't think I love *her!*"

"Well, thank the good Lord," Ida declared, as she stepped spritely into the carriage house, picking pieces of shrubbery out of her blue-white hair. "I was beginning to think you might never figure that out, Zachary Petty, which left me with very little choice but to stick my nose in where it doesn't belong."

Zack was so astonished by the smiling old lady's opening comments that he didn't bother reminding her that, for as long as he'd known her, she'd never demonstrated the slightest reluctance to stick her nose into his business. "You're telling me I'm right?" he exclaimed, both feet hitting the floor with a thud as he sat up straight in his desk chair. "That ridiculous woman doesn't realize I'm in love with her?"

Ida set her pruning shears down on the filing cabinet, then made herself comfortable atop a large cardboard box packed with old books. As she drew off her soiled garden gloves, she lifted one censorious eyebrow at him. "As I hear tell, those three important little words never entered your mind as you listed all the reasons my niece should marry you. Marvelously romantic reasons, such as how you want her to stay home so that she can do all your cooking and cleaning and help you raise a passel of well-behaved little Pettys."

"Hell!" Zack said, raking a frustrated hand through his hair. "How in the devil could she possibly think that's all I wanted to marry her for? Of course I love her! That goes without saying."

Another female voice was quick to answer him. "Nonsense! Where a vulnerable young woman is concerned, nothing goes without saying. Now what, pray tell, do you intend to do about this appalling state of affairs? Three weeks is entirely long enough for all of us to suffer."

Zack's brows rose as he watched Esther Hartcourt enter the carriage house, her pale blue trousers sporting two damp spots at the knees and her tightly wound bun sprouting a variety of twigs, leaves and mulch. Apparently, the good woman felt that desperate situations required desperate measures and had, therefore, joined her sister on a reconnaissance mission. Zack tried, but failed to suppress his grin as he pictured the stiff-necked matriarch crawling on her hands and knees through his shrubbery.

Esther glared down her autocratic nose at Zack, daring him to voice his amusement at her suspiciously disheveled appearance. "Well, my dear?" she persisted, once it became obvious that he was content to tease her with nothing more than a knowing smile. "Can you handle this problem on your own, or will you require our help?"

Ida quickly lended her support to that inquiry. "To see our Emily smile again, we're willing to do most anything."

"Absolutely anything," Esther emphasized firmly.

Zack already knew how much Ida cared for her niece, but until today, he hadn't been aware that Esther shared a similar devotion. The look he gave her conveyed his newfound respect for her, and his voice the gratitude he felt toward them both. "Thank you, ladies, but now that I understand the problem, I'm pretty sure I can handle it myself."

Esther and Ida exchanged relieved glances, then turned back to Zack and smiled. "Mission accomplished," Ida stated in supreme satisfaction, giving her sister an I-told-you-so pat on the shoulder.

Esther pulled a twig out of her hair, rolled her eyes heavenward, then emitted a long-suffering sigh. "Indeed."

At five o'clock on Friday afternoon, Emily succeeded in escaping from Zack's house without his asking the inevitable question, the one she'd been expecting and dreading for the past three weeks. She knew she couldn't postpone the inevitable forever, but because she didn't work for Zack on weekends, at least she'd won herself another two-day reprieve. Unfortunately a hundred days wouldn't change the disheartening fact that she was pregnant.

Of course, Emily reminded herself, she still didn't have scientific confirmation of the condition and she couldn't obtain any until her period was more than a week late, but she didn't need a pregnancy test to tell her what she already knew. A wondrous night of boundless loving such as she'd shared with Zack could have only one result. She'd conceived that night, and now, even though the man she loved thought of their affair as something sordid, their glorious lovemaking had produced a child.

"A beautiful baby girl or boy with parents who will always love it, but not each other," Emily whispered as she mounted the stairs to her bedroom, the anguish she felt whenever she thought about that bleak future deepening the dark shadows beneath her eyes and draining all the remaining color from her cheeks. "I don't know if I'll be able to bear it. I truly don't."

But she had to. As soon as Zack found out she was pregnant, he was going to hold her to her promise. She knew that as surely as she knew that his child was growing in her womb. "Mrs. Zachary Petty. Emily Anne Petty. The great Zoomer Petty, retired football star and his little nonentity of a wife, Emily."

A half hour later, Emily decided she couldn't lie on her bed staring up at the ceiling for the rest of the night. She couldn't afford to skip another meal even if her appetite was nonexistent. As the old maxim said, a pregnant woman was eating for two, and if she continued eating almost nothing, her unborn child would also suffer. Even if she had to force herself, she was going to eat a well-balanced meal, as recommended in the book she'd purchased yesterday on pregnancy and childbirth.

Emily paused on her way down the stairs, hearing the sound of raised voices and the clatter of pots and pans coming from the kitchen. Her aunts were arguing over what dishes were her favorites, and upon hearing the culinary masterpieces each were planning to include on tonight's menu, Emily realized she'd arrived at a wise decision. If she made any attempt to forgo dinner again, as she had for the past two evenings, she got the distinct impression that her aunts were planning to force-feed her.

She was about to lean over the handrail and shout that it wouldn't be necessary for them to go to such extremes when the doorbell rang, and since neither one of the bickering cooks was likely to hear it, Emily answered the summons herself. "May I help you?" she asked. Their caller was a deliveryman who'd obviously been given the wrong address by a local florist.

"Are you Miss Emily Hartcourt?" the man inquired politely, and when she said yes, he thrust a long white box into her startled hands, then walked off before she could find the wherewithal to offer him a tip.

"Flowers? For me?" she asked the empty front hallway, and getting no answer, she set the box down on the entry table and lifted off the top. Inside were two dozen of the most lovely long-stemmed red roses she'd ever seen and a small white card. The card contained a short poem, and though it wasn't signed, Emily's eyes widened in shock when she read it.

"Roses are red. I pray you see these as my first advance, in what shall be our hearts-and-flowers romance."

"Zack?" she whispered incredulously, but she wasn't given any more time to contemplate the farfetched notion that a man who despised her had just sent her flowers. The doorbell rang again, and this time, the deliveryman standing outside handed her a huge heart-shaped box of chocolate candy. As the other fellow had, he disappeared down the walk in the wink of an eye before she could offer him a tip.

Stepping back inside the doorway, Emily opened the accompanying card, her fingers trembling as she read the heart-stopping message written there in a bold masculine scrawl. "Sweets to the sweet, and there is no woman sweeter than my very own Em."

"My very own Em," she repeated in bemusement, happy tears gathering in her eyes as she reflected on the possessive connotation of those words. Or was she reading more into their meaning than what was actually meant?

She was still trying to decide when the doorbell rang again. This time she didn't open it to a single deliveryman, but two of them, and each man was pushing a dolly. "What on earth...!" she exclaimed, and the tallest of the two pointed at the distinctive logo on the boxes strapped securely to the wheeled, metal frame.

"A computer?" she managed to inquire past the growing lump in her throat.

"Top-of-the-line word-processing equipment and letter-quality printer," the man elaborated. "So where would you like it?"

Before Emily could respond, Zack stepped into view and suggested, "I think we should set it up next to mine in the carriage house, love. That way, we'll be able to work side by side and toss ideas back and forth if one of us gets writer's block. How does that sound to you?"

"I...I...think that sounds fine," Emily stammered, still not sure she'd put the correct meaning on all these marvelous presents, but positive Zack was gazing at her as if her opinion was the only thing that mattered to him.

Emily was unaware that she was staring back at him in exactly the same way, but her adoring gaze proved to Zack that she still loved him, and that knowledge made him so happy that he felt like shouting his joy to the world. Instead he gave the deliverymen instructions on the best route to take through his heavily wooded backyard, then told them all about the electrical hookups he'd installed along the rear wall of the carriage house. Both men departed shortly thereafter, but when Zack turned around, intending to resume his romantic conquest of Emily, she was no longer standing in the doorway.

Unlike his future wife, Zack felt no compunction about entering a neighbor's house without an invitation. As far as he was concerned, that melting look he'd seen in Emily's eyes was invitation enough and the strength of that gaze carried him straight through the door, down the front hallway and into the darkened parlor, where some sixth sense told him she would be waiting.

She was, but to his consternation, she didn't appear that thrilled to see him. "I don't know how you know, but you do, don't you?" she accused bitterly, the moment he came close enough to take her in his arms. "You know that I'm pregnant!"

Of course he knew that, had known it ever since he'd struggled back to awareness from the most intense soul-shattering moment of his life. But he also knew that, for a highly intelligent woman, his Emily sometimes indulged in some highly convoluted thinking. In the brief amount of time it had taken him to dispatch the deliverymen, she'd managed to convince herself that he was showering all this attention on her, not for her sake, but for the sake of the baby.

In two steps, Zack was standing directly in front of her with his hands curled around her slender shoulders. "I love you, Emily," he murmured solemnly over the top of her bent head, giving her the words she'd been silently asking for every time she'd looked at him for the past three weeks, and when she glanced up at him with wide hopeful eyes, he began reciting all the flowery poetry he could remember, which to his supreme chagrin, wasn't much.

From Lord Byron, he pleaded, "'Maid of Athens, ere we part, give, oh give me...uh...um...'"

From Robert Browning, he urged more confidently, "'Grow old along with me! The best is yet to be.'"

At that moment, he was inspired by the infamous lines that Browning's wife, Elizabeth, had written: "'How do I love thee? Let me count the ways. Uh...um...'"

Then, with a last, less than fruitful search of his memory banks, he burst forth with a powerful line from King Lear: "'Her voice was ever soft, gentle, and low, an excellent thing in a woman'!"

Even though her ears were still ringing, Emily managed to keep a straight face as she clasped one hand over her heart and murmured dreamily, "At long last, I've finally found the man of my dreams, a man who whispers romantic poetry into my delicate ears. I greatly fear that I might swoon."

"Swoon away, babe," Zack encouraged, his arms reaching out to drag her against him at the exact moment her legs gave way beneath her. "When it comes to catching fainting damsels, we Prince Charming types have garnered some great stats."

Emily's loving smile told him he'd already won top honors for rushing a woman off her romantic feet, and when he'd finished kissing her, her eyes told him that he'd just won the most coveted award of all. "Mr. Petty, will you please marry me?"

Brow cocked, he demanded suspiciously, "You're not just proposing marriage because you know I'm going to have a baby, are you?"

"No, Zack," she assured him, resting her head against his broad chest. "I love you for yourself alone."

"Ditto," Zack murmured as he lifted her chin and claimed her mouth once more.

As soon as she'd made certain that the kitchen door was closed, Ida turned to Esther with a triumphant expression on her face. "See? It's not the words, sister, but how they're spoken, and when it came to saying things right, my John was just as romantic as your Bill.''

''Humph,'' Esther declared with a snort, but both women were smiling, and they kept on smiling all through dinner.

Epilogue

Emily managed to snap her eighteen-month-old son, Matthew, into a pair of lightweight cotton rompers before he could toddle out of reach, then she searched around her ankles for the boy's identical twin brother, Michael, who ten seconds earlier had been trying to unbuckle the strap on her sandals. "Now where on earth could he have got to?" she murmured under her breath, blowing the damp curls sticking to her hot forehead away from her eyes as she bent down to check beneath the kitchen table and counters.

"Michael," she called, when she couldn't find the boy in any of his usual hiding places. "Come out, come out, wherever you are. It's time for us to go to the park."

"He's probably in the potato bin," Angela declared knowledgeably as she and her father entered the kitchen.

"My guess would be the broom closet," Zack countered, but when they checked those locations both of them were proved wrong.

Matthew clapped his hands to draw everyone's misplaced attention back to himself, and when his distracted parents finally glanced down at him, he announced sagely, "Telpone."

In unison, Zack and Emily turned to the family interpreter in the hopes that she could cast some light on this unintelligible bit of information, and Angela emitted a long-suffering sigh. "Ah, Dad, he's in the study using the phone again."

Emily giggled and Zack shot her a smoldering look before he strode swiftly down the hallway. "If you think that long-distance call he made to Paris last week was so darned funny, you can pay the next phone bill when it comes due."

Patently unmoved by her husband's empty threat, Emily picked up the wicker picnic basket, then bent down with her free arm to lift Matthew. As soon as she had his diaper-padded bottom settled on her right hip, she said, "Okay, Angel, let's you and I head out to the car. By the time your dad retrieves Michael, we'll be all set to go."

Angela, who had spent most of the morning complaining that, since the arrival of her two baby brothers, it now took their family forever to get ready to go anywhere, looked over at the stack of equipment that still had to be loaded into the station wagon before they could start having any fun. She began filling her arms with as much stuff as she could carry, but unfortunately after taking two steps, she lost her grip on the plastic bag of disposal diapers and it tumbled to the floor. "Da...rn it!" she exclaimed angrily. "If those two would just use the potty like they're supposed to, we wouldn't need all these diapers! I think you and Dad are much too easy on them!"

Emily remembered back to the day when a three-year-old Angela had suddenly declared herself ready to use the bathroom facilities, and chuckled. "Yup," she agreed dryly. "We definitely should be firmer."

"By their age, I was already reading," Angela reminded her, using the smug matriarchal tone she'd adopted as soon as her brothers had gotten old enough to smile at her and she'd realized what a strong influence she could have on their upbringing. "And I never ran away all the time the way Michael does."

Emily grinned. "No," she agreed. "You always thought it would be much better to drive."

Angela frowned as she grasped hold of the sack of diapers, unwilling to discuss her own youthful foibles. "C'mon, Mom. Let's get going," she urged impatiently. "We've been standing around here all day."

Carrying a wide-eyed Michael on his shoulders, Zack strode past his scowling daughter. "Yeah, Mom," he declared, sending his wife a triumphant look as he scooped up their cooler, picnic basket and the large diaper bag. "Stop holding up the show."

As she trailed behind her husband and daughter, Emily shook her head over the blatant injustices mothers were oftentimes expected to endure, a feeling that intensified when she wasn't the one who came to a dead halt the instant they were all out the front door. "Who's holding up the show now?" she demanded indignantly.

"The boys in blue," Zack informed her, pointing with his overburdened arm to the squad car screeching to a halt in their driveway.

Emily stepped around her husband in time to see two policemen running toward them across the lawn, their hands poised over their leather holsters. "Is something wrong, officer?" she queried anxiously.

The two cops exchanged startled looks, then the tallest of them, a middle-aged man with a craggy face, replied, "That was going to be our question, ma'am. We just got an emergency 911 call that was traced to this address."

"You're kidding!" Emily exclaimed in surprise. Then, realizing who could be responsible for dialing the rescue squad, she groaned, "Oh, no. It must have been Michael."

"Sorry, officers." Zack grimaced and stepped forward to apologize. "I'm afraid there's been a slight mistake here. The call probably did come from our house, but there's no emergency."

The second officer, a broad-chested young man with piercing brown eyes immediately said, "You do realize, sir, that making a crank phone call to 911 is considered a felony?"

"Oh, Lord, my baby boy is already a felon," Emily moaned, wondering what else could possibly happen today that could top this embarrassing episode, especially since she was acutely aware that where her irrepressible family was concerned, anything was possible.

The first policeman studied his two infantile suspects, then started to chuckle. "One of those little guys called?"

Zack pointed to the smiling towhead who was sitting on his shoulders. "This is your perpetrator, officer. I'm afraid that lately he's developed quite an obsession for touch-tone dialing. I'm also afraid we caught him using our phone just a few minutes ago."

The younger man glared at the guilty toddler, then declared tongue-in-cheek, "We usually make an arrest in these cases as a deterrent to others who might not understand the seriousness of this offense."

As soon as Emily heard that, she set Matthew down on the grass and dropped everything else she was carrying so that she could reach up for Michael. Once she had her delinquent son secured in her arms, she held him out to the policeman. "Go ahead," she advised them solemnly. "Do your duty and take him in."

Zack's eyes lit up as if his wife had just come up with a capital idea, and he gave the men a nod of encouragement. "Go ahead and make your arrest, boys. Our son has to learn that laws are made to be obeyed, and a short stint in the slammer should do it for him. Of course, it may take us a while to raise his bail, but we'll get around to it eventually. Won't we, Em? Say in about three hours."

"Four," Emily corrected. "At least four."

Instantly both men backed away from the wiggling boy Emily was holding out to them. The first one shook his head. "These folks sound much too anxious to me, Johnson. I say we leave him in the custody of his parents.''

Officer Johnson quickly agreed with his partner's assessment. ''Right you are, Palmer. We're outa here.''

Thirty seconds later, the squad car was reversing down the drive. Sighing, Emily and Zack watched it go, then looked at each other and grinned. ''Appears as if we're stuck with the little criminal,'' Zack said with a mock sigh, then shifted his gaze to include Angela and Matthew. ''Think you can handle a twenty-year sentence with this wild gang?''

Emily lifted her nose in the air and replied. ''All this wayward trio needs is a crafty gang leader, and I'm good, Mr. Petty. Real good.''

Zack gave his wife an adoring look. ''Mrs. Petty, you're not only good. You're the best.''

* * * * *

SILHOUETTE® *Desire*™

COMING NEXT MONTH

AVAILABLE NOW:

"INDULGE A LITTLE" SWEEPSTAKES

HERE'S HOW THE SWEEPSTAKES WORKS

NO PURCHASE NECESSARY

To enter each drawing, complete the appropriate Official Entry Form or a 3" by 5" index card by hand-printing your name, address and phone number and the trip destination that the entry is being submitted for (i.e., Walt Disney World Vacation Drawing, etc.) and mailing it to: Indulge '91 Subscribers-Only Sweepstakes, P.O. Box 1397, Buffalo, New York 14269-1397.

No responsibility is assumed for lost, late or misdirected mail. Entries must be sent separately with first class postage affixed, and be received by: 9/30/91 for the Walt Disney World Vacation Drawing, 10/31/91 for the Alaskan Cruise Drawing and 11/30/91 for the Hawaiian Vacation Drawing. Sweepstakes is open to residents of the U.S. and Canada, 21 years of age or older as of 11/7/91.

For complete rules, send a self-addressed, stamped (WA residents need not affix return postage) envelope to: Indulge '91 Subscribers-Only Sweepstakes Rules, P.O. Box 4005, Blair, NE 68009.

© 1991 HARLEQUIN ENTERPRISES LTD.

DIR-RL

"INDULGE A LITTLE" SWEEPSTAKES

HERE'S HOW THE SWEEPSTAKES WORKS

NO PURCHASE NECESSARY

To enter each drawing, complete the appropriate Official Entry Form or a 3" by 5" index card by hand-printing your name, address and phone number and the trip destination that the entry is being submitted for (i.e., Walt Disney World Vacation Drawing, etc.) and mailing it to: Indulge '91 Subscribers-Only Sweepstakes, P.O. Box 1397, Buffalo, New York 14269-1397.

No responsibility is assumed for lost, late or misdirected mail. Entries must be sent separately with first class postage affixed, and be received by: 9/30/91 for the Walt Disney World Vacation Drawing, 10/31/91 for the Alaskan Cruise Drawing and 11/30/91 for the Hawaiian Vacation Drawing. Sweepstakes is open to residents of the U.S. and Canada, 21 years of age or older as of 11/7/91.

For complete rules, send a self-addressed, stamped (WA residents need not affix return postage) envelope to: Indulge '91 Subscribers-Only Sweepstakes Rules, P.O. Box 4005, Blair, NE 68009.

© 1991 HARLEQUIN ENTERPRISES LTD.

DIR-RL

INDULGE A LITTLE—WIN A LOT!

Summer of '91 Subscribers-Only Sweepstakes

OFFICIAL ENTRY FORM

This entry must be received by: Sept. 30, 1991
This month's winner will be notified by: Oct. 7, 1991
Trip must be taken between: Nov. 7, 1991—Nov. 7, 1992

YES, I want to win the Walt Disney World® vacation for two. I understand the prize includes round-trip airfare, first-class hotel and pocket money as revealed on the "wallet" scratch-off card.

Name _____

Address_____ Apt. _____

City _____

State/Prov. _____ Zip/Postal Code _____

Daytime phone number _____
(Area Code)

Return entries with invoice in envelope provided. Each book in this shipment has two entry coupons—and the more coupons you enter, the better your chances of winning!

© 1991 HARLEQUIN ENTERPRISES LTD.   CPS-M1

INDULGE A LITTLE—WIN A LOT!

Summer of '91 Subscribers-Only Sweepstakes

OFFICIAL ENTRY FORM

This entry must be received by: Sept. 30, 1991
This month's winner will be notified by: Oct. 7, 1991
Trip must be taken between: Nov. 7, 1991—Nov. 7, 1992

YES, I want to win the Walt Disney World® vacation for two. I understand the prize includes round-trip airfare, first-class hotel and pocket money as revealed on the "wallet" scratch-off card.

Name _____

Address_____ Apt. _____

City _____

State/Prov. _____ Zip/Postal Code _____

Daytime phone number _____
(Area Code)

Return entries with invoice in envelope provided. Each book in this shipment has two entry coupons—and the more coupons you enter, the better your chances of winning!

© 1991 HARLEQUIN ENTERPRISES LTD.   CPS-M1